*Play Me the Song of Death*

*Books by Dale Pierce*
PLAY ME THE SONG OF DEATH
RIOT AT THE GARDEN
TORERO! TORERO!
THE WIND BLOWS DEATH

# Play Me the Song of Death

### A Novel by

## Dale Pierce

Exposition Press      Smithtown, New York

To Don Eduardo Miura of Sevilla and the bravest, deadliest bulls in the world

# CONTENTS

# 1

# THE VINDICTIVE

The Huelva bullring was rocked on its very foundation by the loud and vulgar protests of four thousand enraged Spaniards. They were venting their frustration as a single unit against young Cristo Cruz, who danced away from the bull he was facing, unable to control either his feet or his own fears. It had not been a good day for him, not at all, and the audience, who had paid double prices in order to see him perform, let him know what they thought of being let down. The bullfight fans had seemingly blended together, forming one lone monster, rather than a group of outraged individuals, threatening to devour the shaken matador alive, as punishment for his failure to accomplish with the snorting Miura bull.

Yet amid the rain of cushions and debris, which came hurtling from the stands, one man was enjoying it all. He stood apart from the howling throng, absorbed by the mob reaction, but strangely detached from it. Dressed not in the clothes of the common man, but the sparkling uniform of the bullfighting profession, the silk and gold lamé suit of lights, Jaime Sublaran watched from behind the protection of the wooden barrier that separated him both from the golden sand, which contained the enraged fighting bull, and the stands filled with angry spectators above.

For the past nine years, he had been king of the world—the bullfighting world anyway, his monarchy extending throughout Spain, Portugal, and Latin America. He was only thirty, but he looked much older, the pressures of being the top matador in his profession aging him early. Yet in spite of the fears and the constant dangers, he had never been gored, not even scratched, proving he was the master of masters, just as the newspapers and the posters advertising his fights proclaimed. King of the world! At least it had been that way until the April fair in Sevilla. At that time, a new knight had arrived on the scene, one who proclaimed to be the deserving ruler of the bullfighting realm, challenging the right of Jaime Sublaran to sit upon the royal throne.

The newcomer's name was Cristo Cruz, an upstart from the slums of Triana, a sleazy suburb of Sevilla, who in his rising to sudden stardom had pulled not only himself but his entire family out of the gripping claws of starvation into the limelight of fame. He had always been branded as good, an inexperienced, yet capable matador who showed promise in all phases of bullfighting. With the big *capoté*, his opening passes were elegant; with the smaller *muleta*, the red, flannel cape, he was brave and dominating; and with the kill, he was as deadly as Sublaran himself. For over three years, he'd hung around the smaller plazas and pueblos, fighting whatever animals the promoters pitted him against, whenever and wherever he could. Then, at the big Sevilla fair, his great break came when the Colombian matador, Santiago Dominguez, was gored, leaving two unfulfillable contracts to his name during the two weeks of consecutive, daily bullfights, and the need of a substitute to fill in for him. Cristo Cruz had been that man, and fill in he did, cutting the ears off of every bull he faced, winning the highest of awards and the admiration of all who saw him. Suddenly, the twenty-year-old up-and-coming star had arrived. That was when Jaime Sublaran took notice.

His long-secure throne was now threatened. The perfect matador who knew no rivals had suddenly been accorded one, a realization which hardly served to make him happy. For long hours he worried about the situation, his pride hurt, his composure failing fast, fearful to the point of outright panic that he would have to share the spotlight with another. It couldn't happen. A man of his ego would not allow such a thing, meaning there could be only one alternative. He, Jaime Sublaran, would challenge the upstart to a series of mano a mano corridas, as they were called in the trade lingo, hand to hand, competitive bullfights in which the two of them alternated together, in an effort to outdo the other, proving beyond any shade of a doubt who was the rightful claimant to the title of world's greatest matador.

Their first meeting was signed for Huelva, a tiny, unimportant city known mainly for its mines and port, some seventy miles from Sevilla. Solitary, tourist scorned, it seemed an unlikely setting for the initial bullfight between such rivals, for in its long history, only four important events had ever occurred there.

First, Huelva became known as the port from which Columbus set sail for the new world, the statue in the town square serving as a reminder that even in this ignored Spanish city, a historical footnote had been made. The town, however, would have to wait more than two long centuries before another landmark would come across its fetid soil, this time in the form of an unidentified body, drifting ashore during the heat of World War II. Hardly a noteworthy incident at first sight, but this water-bogged corpse, who to this day remains nameless, was carrying in its pockets forged information which embarrassingly misled the Germans about the Allied plans for invading Europe, causing a major blow to the changing Axis power destiny. The third and fourth great happenings stemming from Huelva surround the bullring, as two great matadors, Manuel and Miguel Baez, were born there, names which under the alias of "El Litri" would become famous in the world of sunlight and horned death, surpassed only decades later when Jaime Sublaran erased their memory with his own brand of courage before the bulls.

Four things and four things only had Huelva to boast about, though Sublaran liked the city and owned a huge mansion on the outskirts of town. Little did the people know that as they booed themselves into a frenzy over the failure of Cristo Cruz, incident number five was about to take place.

"It doesn't look good for him," Sublaran smirked, now reassured that his position was safe. "If this is all Cristo Cruz has to offer, I'm not particularly worried."

Sublaran's manager and part-time photographer, Paco Solorzano, nodded, but said nothing, tapping his camera handle against the wooden fence, his eyes still on the action. During a decade spent handling business affairs for the flightly ace of matadors, he knew that no matter how greatly the newcomer failed, Sublaran would still not be satisfied. Within the mind and heart of the arrogant matador rested both a feeling of insecurity and burning hatred for anyone who overshadowed him, making him look bad in either his professional or private life. It was no secret that although he smirked at Cristo Cruz, relishing his failure, the poison had been stirred alive. Solorzano knew where it had begun, in Sevilla when the fans first hailed the youngster as a challenger to the spot of number one, but where it would end, he did not know. That was what bothered him, why he felt a cold, hard twisting deep within his stomach, as he heard his matador's words, for he did not know the answer, nor did he want to find out.

Another disappointed howl rose from the stands in unison as Cristo Cruz went in for the kill, missing his mark. The sword hit bone, reflecting off the animal's shoulder blades rather than burying in the spot between them, sinking into the heart or aorta, bringing instant death. One could almost read the words escaping from the young man's own lips, uttering curses out of frustration, due to his own failure and the crowd's inability to understand the pressures that brought it about. Wearily, he flapped his cape a few more times, backed up to reposition himself, and aimed the sword again.

"It isn't going to work," Sublaran hissed from the passageway, his eyes glistening in hate, delighted at seeing the newcomer brought down low, humbled before him like a broken idol. "It isn't going to work."

A scream broke off the rest of his words as a few yards away, he saw the bull swerve inward, ripping the cape out of the bullfighter's hand. Cristo Cruz was shoved aside, running, trying to escape the bull, which hooked at the shredded red lure on the ground, the sword protruding from the side of its neck, barely penetrating. With one shake of the bull's head, the instrument fell out, and the crowd responded with another shower of abuse, both verbal and physical, flinging cushions, orange peels, and paper cups.

"Son of a bitch," Cruz swore, taking another cape and sword from a ring attendant. "The bull's made of cement. Why won't the damned thing die?"

Again, he went to the bull, the cheers he'd dreamed of earlier now only a faded sparkle of hope, drowned out by the waves of protest from the ignited fans, who were insulting not only him, but his family, his chosen profession, and his abilities. He was tired, beaten. He wanted to finish it, go back to the hotel, and wait for another day with another bull, in another city, when he could regain his lost honor.

The bull was waiting for him, studying him, watching him come. It was mocking him, like the people, like Sublaran, enjoying his agony, loving it as they tore him down together. He raised the sword and threw himself forward, again missing his mark. The sword hurt his wrist as it bounced off the bone, jamming it. He shook with pain, biting his lip, but he wasn't quitting. He wouldn't give any of them the satisfaction, particularly his rival. They wouldn't see him admit defeat, not even if it meant taking a horn wound.

For a moment, Cristo Cruz turned to face the wooden barrier, where Sublaran observed him. Though they were a good distance away, their eyes seemed to lock, yet each of them vibrated something entirely different. Cruz's eyes spoke only of frustration, a shrugging off of disappointment which found security in the fact that somehow, somewhere, he would have another chance, while Sublaran's eyes blazed, aflame with hatred that went beyond either simple contempt or satisfaction. It was more than just anger. It was a murderous, insane bloodlust, as if he wished his rival to be torn to pieces on the horns of the bull that challenged him.

"Oh, I know," Cruz muttered as he retrieved his sword. "Your kingdom is safe for the moment, number one. Enjoy it while you can. It won't last. I'll live to take it away from you."

Turning, he flapped the bull into position with his cape, then rose yet another time, taking careful aim, citing down the glistening steel sword blade. "I'll give you reason to hate me," he cursed, biting down, so the words escaped like the air-hiss of a cobra ready to strike. "I'll give you reason . . ."

The horn caught him between the legs, throwing him into the air as he attempted to make the kill. He toppled to the sand hard, rolling away, rising only when he knew it was safe. The other bullfighters had come to his rescue, moving in to lure the bull away from him. Sublaran had not been one of them. He'd maintained his stiff, uncaring position against the fence, as if hoping the bull had gored him.

"Son of a bitch," Cruz cried aloud, the frustration overcoming him. "Son of a bitch. Son of a bitch."

Tears were welling up in his eyes, overflowing, not from pain, but anger. He hated the bull, which made him look foolish by refusing to die. He hated Sublaran, the jealous, high-riding bastard! He hated the public for turning on him, and he hated himself for ever becoming a bullfighter. In his dismay, he refused to look at his rival, for he knew the satisfaction and security he'd find in those mocking features. For brief seconds, he toyed with the idea of leaving the bull, running up to Sublaran, and driving the sword into his heart, stopping his mockery, stopping his enjoyment, then climbing into the stands, killing as many of the agitators as he could, before the Civil Guards stopped him.

"Assassin! Butcher! Shameless bastard! Coward! Is this what we've waited for? May you burn in hell, you filthy bungler! You're no matador de toros!"

The insults boomed like the gunfire of war, filling the air, echoing off the walls of the packed bullring, rebounding, falling to center upon the sweating, battered matador, who was lining up once more, in an attempt to finally end the ordeal. Only now he was far less reserved, his composure failing him entirely. He knew he had to get it right. He was running out of time. He had to pull it off. Things were getting too far out of hand to be carried much further. There was a riot brewing all around him.

"This time he'll do it," Sublaran noted without any further betrayal of emotions. "Why not? He's already ruined everything."

Before the words left his mouth, Cristo Cruz flung himself over the horns, sighing in relief as he finally felt the sword sink in, an inch at a time, up to the hilt, where his hand touched the fur on the animal's back. Turning, he profiled in mock triumph, but the token ripple of applause he expected was not to be found, only another round of jeers, more violent than before. From his viewpoint, the thrust appeared to be perfect, but when the animal moved, he saw what had escaped his attention, yet had been seen by the entire audience, infuriating them further.

The sword, rather than going straight inward and down to nick the heart, had bent, slicing sideways, so the tip of the blade protruded from the bull's neck. Instead of dying the swift, bloodless death from a well-placed thrust, it was hemorrhaging, dying an undeserved, grotesque death that nobody wanted to see, rounding out his failure on the most unfortunate note of all.

Through his tear-stung eyes, Cristo Cruz watched the animal roll to its side like a fallen tree hitting the dirt, blood bursting from its mouth and nostrils in an ugly red foam. The ultimate disgrace, a sloppy, inaccurate thrust more befitting a butcher or stockyard killer than a matador de toros who was supposed to show promise of becoming one of the best toreros in the field. The crowd was letting him know it now more than ever. Amid their insults even more seat cushions, half-eaten food, and paper cups came flying into the ring, covering the sand to make it look more like a circular junk heap than a bullring. Blindly, the young matador staggered back behind the fence, feeling the humiliation and the pain. He had failed, not just simply, but completely, an absolute disaster from start to finish, the realization of lost honor hitting him in the face like a wet towel. Unable to hold back any longer, he put his head in his arms, resting on the wooden barrier, and wept in bitterness. His dreams of triumph and glory were gone, crushing him as they collapsed.

From a spot not far away, Jaime Sublaran studied the spectacle with amused interest. Then, as if spurred by a certain malignant demon sitting unseen on his shoulder, he nudged his manager, pointing toward the scene.

"Solorzano, get me some pictures of this. I want to remember what happened to this fraud who thought he could rival me."

Obediently, the sidekick took a few steps forward, so he now stood in front of the matador, partially blocking his view. For an instant, the movie camera whirled into play, capturing the incident for all eternity. Feeling his task was completed, Solorzano lowered the camera and raised his eyebrows questioningly at his matador. Sublaran, however, exploded, his face growing hard, as biting as the sudden gust of sea wind which had swept through the plaza, and his lips curled into a canine snarl.

"Keep filming, damn you! I'll tell you when I want you to stop!"

Without bothering to question the command, Solorzano turned the camera again on the young matador, who was taking his failure so harshly.

Solorzano was so busy that he failed to notice Jaime Sublaran standing behind him, his face seeming to alter in shape and texture as the shades of twilight swept over the arena, gleaming with a flickering yellow light of its own, like the candle in an American jack-o-lantern going through its death throes before burning out. The familiar, unemotional sadness in his eyes, which had been his trademark since the early years, had undergone a sudden, frightening transition, reflecting not mere satisfaction, but lust over his rival's failure, a vindictive sparkle hinting insanity in its most sinister form. No words escaped his lips, only an animal growl, low and hate-filled, unheard amid the protest of the disappointed patrons in the stands.

Some say that Cristo Cruz went insane at that moment. It was the only logical explanation for what was to happen as he gave the city of Huelva something they'd long remember him by. Even after his gravestone joined the hordes of neglected others and his name became forgotten, for all its promise, he was remembered only for a certain action, which took only a few seconds, but sent him into the blackness of eternity and the statistics of the bullfighting record books. Frantic, babbling words no one could understand, the young matador pulled himself erect from his sobbing, submissive position, throwing himself upon one of the armed Civil Guards standing closest to him, yanking his miniature submachine gun away from him.

Everyone saw it. Those who remained in the stands to boo the matador and those who had risen to leave all turned when they heard the scream, above the rapping of the machine gun, as Cristo Cruz put it beneath his jaw and pulled the trigger. Over in a flash, the matador's already lifeless body hurtling backward, against the concrete wall, then downward, into the sand like the bull that had died so violently just minutes before. Everything had happened in that batting of an eyelid, but the impact of what took place that afternoon would never truly die, though the people present would try to bury it often enough. Like an unstaked vampire, it would rise again in their memories, repeating itself through bar talk, gossip, dreams. Cristo Cruz had made himself famous in a way he neither intended nor would have accepted had he maintained full control of his reasoning. In killing himself, he had given Huelva the fifth event to record in its history books, the blackest and bloodiest incident of all.

While this happened, Jaime Sublaran watched smugly, grinning as if by some demonic power he had sent an angel of hell to take possession of the beaten matador, taunting him toward self-destruction. Indeed, he looked well pleased, slowly slipping away as he watched the crowd form around the dead torero's body, unable to contain himself any longer, his grin converting into a full, leering smile. Above the glitter of his white teeth, boasting happily of his rival's sudden death, his eyes likewise sparkled. For behind their circled, brooding sadness had been ignited a burning light from the flames of the fires of hell!

In his moment of macabre triumph, while his cameraman whirled away recording the violent climax to the afternoon, Sublaran didn't realize that in the front row of stands, someone else, an American tourist who had come to Huelva just to see this particular fight, was taking his picture.

# 2

# SOUL OF EVIL

Jaime Sublaran was dead, gored in the Plaza de Toros de los Ventas in Madrid, during the famed San Isidro Fair, two years after the Huelva tragedy. The goring had been the most hideous in the history of bullfighting, or so all the experts claimed, even more nightmarish than the skull-crushing injury that killed Manuel Granero back in 1922. For all who saw, either live or through the news telecast, it was truly a sickening sight, turning the stomachs of even the most sadistic men.

Sublaran had been fighting to the tune of "La Ultima Estocada," played by the bullring band. The press had nicknamed it "Sublaran's Theme" because he always insisted on having it played whenever he was performing well. It inspired him so much that he made sure he always carried copies of the composition so the band could play the melody, even if they'd never heard of it before, regardless of the bullring. In a way, it was appropriate for him to die with the song ringing in his ears, as in English the translation simply means "The Last Sword Thrust," something the matador, unfortunately, did not get to make that afternoon.

He was dancing in front of the horns, working close as he always did, when the bull swerved inward, driving a horn deep into his groin. Had it been that wound alone, the matador surely would have survived, but instead of being tossed clear, away from the horns, sailing over the animal's head, the bull threw him in such a way that he fell flat on his back, giving the bull time to crash down on him.

10

Perhaps Sublaran realized in those last seconds that he was a dead man. Maybe he thought of reasons why, what he had done wrong to cause the accident, or of his long career without such a mishap. Was it his palacelike house, the blue skies of southern Spain which he would never see again, or perhaps the late Cristo Cruz, who most assuredly looked on from heaven, laughing just as Sublaran had laughed two years before when he put the gun to his neck and fired? No one knew for sure, nor would they ever find out, for the horned giant bore down on its prone target, catching the matador beneath his jawbone, close in location to where young Cruz had placed the gun, lifting him upward, spiked on the bull's head as he danced the dead man's dance, arms and legs flopping foolishly in a hornpipe without music, as in its horror, the bullring band had ceased to play. When he was thrown again to the sand, the bull refused to leave him, hooking and tearing at his neck and head, until after several seconds, the other matadors were able to lead it away.

Instantly, ring workers scooped up the matador and carried him from the ring, but he was dead before he reached the infirmary, his face destroyed so completely that Madrid's daily newspaper would have to edit the photo of him being removed from the arena, blocking out the entire upper body from view with the help of an airbrush.

Thus Jaime Sublaran's career as a matador came to an end, but he really didn't need the bull to put him in the grave. The tourist who snapped the picture of the laughing Sublaran, who gloated on the death of Cristo Cruz, had sold it to the international magazine, *Paris Match*. They, in turn, had run it on their front cover and the reaction of the world as a whole had been first disbelief, then disgust. Sublaran, once the idol of the multitudes, was blacklisted, boycotted, and avoided like a flu epidemic. His patrons left him, regarding him no longer as a champion bullfighter, but a sadistic madman. When he stepped into the Madrid arena that final day, he was already defeated, disgraced past any point of humiliation Cristo Cruz could or would ever have known. Yet in spite of all this, he remained unchanged, worsening if anything at all, growing more envious, more vindictive, more cruel.

Many things came out after his death on the horns, gossip for the most part, as follows any celebrity's death. He had been on drugs.

He was an alcoholic. He belonged to a demonic cult. He sold his soul to the devil. He was really the man responsible for a chain of murders in Mexico five years before, guilty of slicing up prostitutes like Jack the Ripper. How much was truth and how much was fabrication would never be known, for it mingled together quickly, forming a gloomy, mythical legend, an obituary as strange and forboding as the late bullfighter himself.

Even in death, Sublaran continued to make news. His body was not buried in Spain, but flown to Ireland, laid to rest amid total indifference, with no mourners, photographers, or newsmen. From the grave, he seemed to rise and violate tradition, for in his will he had specifically refused the traditional send-off given to matadors, a ritual of driving the hearse through town, stopping it at the local bullring, and removing the coffin, so admirers can carry it one last time around the ring before returning it to the car and finally the ground. A last lap in homage to a matador, who supposedly lives for the ultimate glory of being carried around the bullring on the shoulders of the fans, first in triumph, then finally in death. Yet Sublaran had forbidden himself even this tidbit of tradition, an action which brought him no closer to the fans who had turned from him.

For a while, Paco Solorzano, the manager who had captured Cristo Cruz shooting himself on film, on command from his protege, as if Sublaran somehow knew something was going to happen, tried to calm the waves at first, claiming it to all be newspaper gossip, but in time he grew weary, fading from view and away from his lost cause, to take up the profession of sword maker in Huelva. He would later move to Sevilla and remain there when public scorn forced him away, the citizens having had their fill of memories pertaining to Jaime Sublaran.

Over twenty years had passed, slowly, torturously, yet the memory of the matador was never completely erased. Though Huelva, confronted with the reality of the situation, tried hard, it could not. There were always the reminders, the unholy shrines that stood out to keep the dead alive.

One such shrine was the house of Jaime Sublaran, which stood on the outskirts of Huelva, unoccupied and ignored. Scarcely cared for by a distant relative, the palatial home began to crumble, altering outwardly as the years passed on, until it was only a shell of what once had been Sublaran's castle, while he was still alive and respected.

The house had once attracted tourists, who came by train from various parts of Spain to stare at the mansion through the iron gates. What went on behind them became the subject of much gossip and slander once the owner had died, but while he lived and still enjoyed the height of glory, his home stood out, intentionally created to show the world what Jaime Sublaran did with the fortune he risked his life to earn.

The mansion had been painstakingly constructed, designed in the style of a Confederate plantation, so it would be unique in all of Spain. It had been Sublaran's brainstorm, for with this phenomenal construction, he received even more publicity and once again was cast into the limelight. Either in front of the horns or away from them, Jaime Sublaran was certain to be the center of attention.

When the matador's career plunged downward and his ultimate destruction came, followed by the great scandals, the house he left behind went from being a shrine for a demigod to a desecrated temple. Had it not been for the fence, the fact that the house's new renter was a high-ranking clergyman, and the general aura of forboding that surrounded the mansion, the people of Huelva would have more than likely blown the mansion to rubble, freeing themselves of the last reminder of Jaime Sublaran for good.

It was no secret the people of Huelva were burdened with a tremendous guilt, as they were the ones who had idolized Jaime Sublaran as a conquering hometown hero. He was the man who put their city on the map to a degree that Columbus, the celebrated John Doe corpse, and all the Litris, with their famous dynasty of bullfighters, had never been able to do. When their patron saint turned into a demon, they were confronted with their own sin and the cold realization that they were the ones who had helped make Sublaran famous, likewise sharing a portion of the blame for all that happened.

When the house went on sale, there were understandably no buyers. The owner wanted nothing to do with it, for in his mind he saw it as a house of "bad shadow," like the gypsies in nearby Sevilla would say, a house full of demons, the evil of its original owner living on past the grave. Even the fence surrounding the property became an uneasy sign of superstitious rumor, leaving those who passed wondering why it had been put there to begin with: to keep someone out or to keep something inside?

The clergyman didn't stay long, and in desperation the house was offered again as a boarding home, but only rarely was it occupied. For one thing, people seldom came to Huelva anymore. The glory of the past had departed, barring certain signs that only hinted that things had once been different. For another, no one wanted to have anything to do with the memory of Jaime Sublaran.

For those who did rent the house, there was nothing out of the ordinary, barring one incident where an American student went mad. On drugs before he ever set foot in Spain, no one could logically blame his death on evil spirits. High on a number of pills, he went running down the streets of Huelva, waving a bedsheet and claiming to be Jaime Sublaran. He attempted to fight the cars as though they were bulls. It hadn't been a fair trade, as he was hit by one of them and, naturally, died on the spot. Although the reason for his bizarre behavior was obvious, the peasants and the devout cast knowing glances at each other, blaming the incident on the evil forces that the mysterious matador had left behind.

Still, all the others found the house comfortable, as most knew little or nothing of the previous owner. They were invariably tourists, college students, or the rich, who heard about the house being available for rent by some agency and found the bargain too irresistible. No one confirmed the rumors in the streets, that the spirit of Jaime Sublaran still walked the halls of his former home.

The renters were for the most part vacationers, but Phil Catron was an exception. By no means obscure, his Western novels had made him famous among fans of the genre in the English-speaking world. Aside from making him famous, however, they had hospitalized him with an acute stomach problem, caused by nerves, and his family had grown so concerned they all but forced him to take a rest.

It was his sister and her husband, a professional wrestler holding one of the numerous world titles in the sport, with enough money to spend, who suggested Spain, having heard of Huelva and the mansion when enquiring about a place to stay in Sevilla, at a Phoenix travel agency. Joined by these two, and his brother-in-law's manager, Phil Catron found himself on a plane heading toward Europe for a summer vacation which everyone else anticipated to be a once-in-a-lifetime experience. Certainly in the gigantic house there was room for four people, even, as Catron thought, room enough to be alone. While the others were well intending, they irritated him to no end. They failed to understand the ways of a professional writer and how it was a business, like anything else. It had to be treated that way.

"After all," he mused to himself as the plane soared high above the Atlantic Ocean, "I remember the old, worn-out saying about the road to hell being paved with good intentions."

The road he was following at the moment may not have been a direct route to hell, but for certain it was to a town he'd never heard of and had no real desire to visit.

# 3

# THE CALLING

By all practical standards, the mansion in Huelva would have been considered a dream house. On a regular basis, a maid would come in to clean the many rooms, all lavishly furnished, and the boarder, with only a minimal strain of imagination, could easily project himself into the role of royalty amid the expensive background. It was the study that attracted Phil Catron the most, a quiet place where he could withdraw from the constant supervision and the nagging of the others to be alone and think. He was even considering working again, though he had made no mention of this fact aloud. Since he was in Spain, all he could do was make the best of it, and even he had to admit the locale provided enough material for several stories.

The first time Catron had ever seen Jaime Sublaran was in the study itself, not in ectoplasmic, spirit form, but captured in a massive, framed oil painting that hung across from what had once been the matador's desk. He was not an old man, except for the eyes that stared out, bitter and hard from the cold exterior of his face. There was a certain gloominess about him, his mouth bearing only the hint of a grin, as if to hide a well-protected secret. Yet there was something else, an aura which no one word could describe. This pertained to the matador's soul, which seemed to peek through the cocky exterior. Brutal, egotistical, cruel. In all accounts, he must have been an interesting man, and according to the stories circulated, not a very nice one.

The painting showed Sublaran dressed in the *traje de luces*, the

16

traditional suit of lights worn by all matadors, made up of silk and gold spangles. This particular costume was gold ornamented on black silk, which made the matador seem all the more dark and brooding. Obviously, he was meant to be making his entrance into the bull-ring in the opening march across the sand, for his decorative parade cape was slung over his left shoulder, his free arm and hand out-stretched accepting the applause from row after row of dotted heads intended to represent spectators in the background. Still, there was something more, something different, but he couldn't place it.

Previously, Catron's experience with bullfighting had been limited to a handful of bullfights in Nogales, Mexico, some 180 miles from his home. The city, a sleepy border town, seldom had top calibre fights in its entire history, and had only produced one matador of any real merit, a local hero named Silviano Tanori. The ring was small, the bulls were smaller, and the reputations of many matadors contracted there were even smaller still. Aside from these spur of the moment travels to Nogales, for lack of anything better to do on a Sunday afternoon, he had only one other memory concerning the bullfight. That was in an old Italian Western film called *The Mercenary*.

The film had featured Jack Palance as the villain, a mean, curly-haired type whose badness had been far more vividly portrayed than the subtle implications of Jaime Sublaran. The hero, on the other hand, was an obscure Italian actor, who slipped his memory. To avoid capture by Palance and crew, he had taken on the disguise of a bullfighting clown, a comic bullfighter putting on his exhibitions of humor for charity, working for the coins tossed to him by the crowd. In the end, it had done him no good, Palance confronting him in the empty bullring, where the unavoidable, climactic gun-fight that always happened in such films took place.

The gunfight scene had been a novelty in itself, due to the musical score. Arranged by another Italian named Ennio Morricone, it was more than just an instrumental song, the highlight being a repeated wail of bullring trumpets, blended in with the repeated strums of a guitar. Then, the two men fired upon each other, and to everyone's surprise, the good guy fell backward, writhing from a bullet wound in the shoulder.

Triumphantly, Palance approached his enemy, convinced of his victory. But just as he was about to fire the fatal second shot, he caught a glimpse of a white carnation pinned to his lapel, which was turning red. In a moment, which Catron had found to be pure cinematic joy, though no one else shared his sense of humor, Palance's gloating smile turned into the sickest look of defeat imaginable, as he realized he had been shot and fell over dead.

For years he had tried unsuccessfully to find a copy of the soundtrack, even contacting an organization in Hollywood noted for putting out Morricone records, but they at the time had no such record in their list. The Ennio Morricone Film Score Society. How unusual. How rare. Maybe if he would have become a composer himself, rather than struggling with writing, he could have had an organization named after him too. Maybe there was hope yet. The Phil Catron Literary Society. There was a nice ring to it.

His instincts were starting to work as he thought about the bullfight and his various exposures to it. There was a story to be made about the art form, or about Jaime Sublaran directly. He could sense it, the calling, an inner voice which alerted him of something that could be turned into a profitable payday. Certainly the late matador had done enough, both good and bad, to merit a book. There were plenty on his early career already, but surprisingly nothing on his life away from the arena or biographical works following his death, as was the case with other celebrities. There was something about him that no one liked to discuss, beyond the episode with Cristo Cruz. That was the call. He knew it now. To find the secret of Jaime Sublaran and put it into print. The others wouldn't like it, not the thought of his working again, particularly on a subject such as this, but he wasn't there to keep them happy. He was living life on what he termed "The Gasoline Plan—Self-Service Only."

Of the group, he hated Dennis Flagstaff, his brother-in-law, the most. He was the pushy sort, like the athletes in high school whom he used to detest so vividly. His sister had seen him wrestling years ago and fallen in love with him. She'd tracked him, like a groupie following a rock star, followed him to the matches, then started dating him. The ultimate result had been marriage, to Catron's displeasure, the only compensation being that although related through wedlock, Flagstaff was no blood relative. They were always at each other's throats, this trip to Spain being a peace offering he knew his sister had been the mastermind behind. Dennis had always been hard to tolerate, but since winning one of the many versions of the World Championship recognized in wrestling, he had become absolutely intolerable.

Next in line was Flagstaff's shadow, Freddie Harmon, his manager, publicity director, and on rare occasions when the promoters could get no one else to fill the card, his tag-team partner. As Phil put it, "If someone was to build a statue to Dennis Flagstaff, it wouldn't be physically correct unless the statue had Freddie Harmon's nose in its ass." While this man didn't consider himself to be the ass-kisser Catron made him out to be, but rather a clever businessman, he was always quick to side in with his protegé on everything and this made him a marked man on the hit list, as far as Phil was concerned. The less said or thought about either of them, the better. They were low-lifes who got paid too much for doing too little. Yet this was the crew his sister had chosen.

That brought his thoughts to Patsy Catron Flagstaff, his little sister. Although they were blood kin, there was a distance between them which had increased with age rather than mellowed. Her marrying Dennis Flagstaff had not eased his feelings either, but worsened them, for fear that his traits and tastes would rub off on her. There were memories, reasons for the dislike, but he could not pinpoint them. They must have existed from somewhere deep in the past, his childhood perhaps, but he could not remember. Therefore they couldn't have been all that important, to be forgotten along the way. His main reason for disliking them all, at this moment, was their combined effort to keep him from writing, not realizing that was an impossibility. Since their jobs were physical, they could leave them anytime they wanted. Since his job was part physical, part mental, he was constantly thinking about his work where ever he went, and nothing could prevent him from doing so, particularly when he felt the calling, as he now did, more strongly than any time in recent memory.

Clearly, his own life was like the life of the hero in *The Mercenary*. By trying to run away from his destiny, he had wound up choosing his own battleground, his own place to make a final stand, though he didn't understand it until the exact moment came. With his own life, he wondered if the ending would be the same. Would he wind up triumphant over the villain, as the good guy had been, or with his luck would he have missed his target entirely, leaving the villain free to walk away unharmed, while he lay dead. Personally, he wished that somehow he could have rewritten the ending to *The Mercenary*, with Jack Palance giving a maniacal laugh then blowing the hero's head off his shoulders, a climax he, himself, would have found gratifying, even if no one else shared his interest.

"I can feel the call," he said aloud, directing his comments to the painting of the matador. "There's a story in you, Jaime Sublaran, a story no one else has told, and that's the one I'm going to write. Do you know what I'm going to do? I'm going to dig up everything I can on you. I'm going to run down your friends, if you had any. I'm going to dig and dig and dig . . . "

He stopped for a moment, words coming into his mind that he wished he hadn't put there.

"I'm going to dig . . . and dig . . . and dig. I'm going to dig my own tunnel to hell. That's what I'll be doing."

There was still something different, something he couldn't finger as it was, about the portrait. He moved closer, staring into the matador's painted eyes. It wasn't his odd expression, nor the color of the suit, but something connected, at the tip of his tongue. For several minutes he examined the painting, like a man searching for hidden words in a crossword puzzle, then the discovery came.

"I'll be damned," he muttered, confirming his diagnosis. "I'll be damned if this isn't the monkey's balls. This is strange, really strange."

On the parade cape, which draped the matador's shoulder, were two repeated designs, yet different from the usual flowers, butterflies, and embroidered pictures of saints which decorated most parade capes worn by bullfighters as they made their entrance into the ring. This particular cape was deliberately designed with a pattern of broken, upside down crosses and circled stars.

"Pentagrams. Signs of a desecrated cross. Omens from hell."

It was then he understood, or at least had found some ground on which to place his foot. The matador was wearing a parade cape adorned with signs of satanism, if indeed the accuracy of the painting was to be believed. But why? Most matadors were practicing Roman Catholics. It was an established fact that even he was familiar with, though he was far from being an established expert on the bullfight.

"Broken crosses," he repeated, trying to combat his imagination, which was now threatening to go overboard. "Pentagrams. Signs of the devil. Who the hell was this guy? What was he? Didn't anyone else notice these things?"

He closed his eyes, imagining Jaime Sublaran as he made his way into the ring, amid the cheering of several thousand fans. They didn't know, didn't realize. To them, it was just another form of decoration. They were ignorant, having no open understanding of such things. All they knew was what they saw in the foreground, that Jaime Sublaran was the greatest matador in the world, at least until he ruined himself with the episode in Huelva, concerning Cristo Cruz. Now this was interesting. He could feel the call, the alarm bells going off inside his head, and he knew what had to be done. At once, he would begin his search in an effort to retrace the trail of the enigmatic matador and try to glue together a picture which was more revealing about his life, than the likeness hung in the study. Maybe this trip would turn out worthwhile after all.

His visions of cash registers going off, of foreign rights for reprints, and possibly a movie, with Ennio Morricone-type music, was shattered by another sound, from far away. The others were returning.

"They aren't going to like this," Catron warned himself, considering everything he knew would happen. "They aren't going to like this at all. The shit is about to hit the fan."

Such didn't really matter, because he had everything he needed. Books, magazines, everything, for he had been lucky enough to have the greatest resource of all at his fingertips—the matador's own house. He even had the study, with its solitude, to do his work, while the portrait of his projected manuscript's subject looked down across from him as if to supervise his work. There was even a desk and a typewriter, which was old and would require some care, such as a cleaning, oiling, and a new ribbon, but that could be arranged. In any case, he was back in business.

"Phil, where are you?" he could hear his sister calling. "We're back. Are you here?"

He closed his eyes, again envisioning Jaime Sublaran, dressed in the black and gold costume, the parade cape draped over his shoulders as he made his way into the ring, the applause of the audience swelling around him. He was their king, at least for the moment, and they were his devoted subjects. He was the greatest matador of all time, ruler of the world, and he was as well aware of that fact as anyone. Yet the only betrayal of this knowledge was a subtle grin, not an ecstatic, victorious smile or loud, mocking laugh. Confident of his position and in his security in maintaining the throne, he stepped forward, across the sand, while music played in the background, and the parade began. The cheers grew so loud, the bullring band, with all their woodwinds, brass, and kettledrums, became unheard, as the roar of adoration filled the air, engulfing everything.

"Phil, are you there?"

"Who the hell cares," came another voice, deeper than Patsy's, more coarse. It belonged to Dennis Flagstaff and vibrated with all his typical charm. "If we're lucky he packed up and went back to Phoenix. . . . "

In his mind, Catron could still see Sublaran marching into the bullring, leading the parade, but something was changing. A film of red was covering the scene, until nothing remained but the crimson glow of blood, as that which had flowed from the bullet hole made in Jack Palance, just before he fell over.

"Phil, are you here," the voice repeated, drawing closer to the open door. Patsy was now in the den, watching him. "Oh, there you are."

Catron opened his eyes, and the first thing he saw was the painting of Jaime Sublaran, looking down from its place on the wall, the face still bearing the grin which had been his trademark for so many years. Somehow though, he felt a new sensation within him, that from somewhere in the unseen, spirit world, the ghost of what had once been the portrait's real-life model, was laughing at him.

"Come on, Phil," Patsy said, moving closer. "Let me show you what I bought today."

Behind her, Dennis Flagstaff and Freddie Harmon peered into the doorway and instantly, Catron found whatever feelings of affection he'd felt for his sister, start to burn within him, a stomach-turning feeling of disgust and hatred for all those around him.

Clearly, a similar feeling must have been felt by Jaime Sublaran when the adoring public turned on him. Like Jack Palance, the matador had unknowingly walked right into his own meeting place with death, the only difference being his was real and not feigned, coming from the horns of a bull and not the creation of stage makeup.

# 4

# THE SEARCH

It had taken Phil Catron only one hour to travel from Huelva to Sevilla, but more than two days to run down the location of Paco Solorzano's dingy sword shop in the heart of Triana, the city's worst slum section, which had ironically been the birthplace of Cristo Cruz. The time span didn't really matter, for he had to get away from the others. They were driving him crazy, smothering him with their concern about his health and his nerves. It seemed strange that they'd all pressured him for so long to join them in Spain so he could relax, only to badger him all the more once he arrived.

As he'd realized upon first hearing the legend of Jaime Sublaran, there was a story to be written, a virtual silver mine which for some reason, every other writer in the world had ignored. For once, it seemed like fate had sided with him, saving him this story, handing it to him as a gift, which he'd turn into a best-seller and start making big money once again on his own, just like his wrestling brother-in-law, whom he hoped would somehow contract for an exhibition match in Europe and be virtually flattened. With a broken jaw, held together with wire, he'd be quiet at least, leaving only two others to nag him about watching his nerves. They, rather than anything else, were prompting him toward the breakdown they feared. Life was a contradiction, as simple as the light of day or the darkness of night, but on the same hand, as complex as the unknown force which created such elements in the beginning.

Now, however, he was away from all that, working once again on the trail of something fiery, tracing it, tracking it down, letting his instincts guide him like a bloodhound toward his goal. He had found the sword shop, ignored, shunned like its owner, and was about to go through the door when something funny ran through his mind.

It was a picture, nothing more, but clear and distinct. He saw a man, standing alone in the center of an empty bullring, dressed in a shining costume of black and gold. The suit of lights, the uniform of the matador, glistening as the spangles reflected the beams of sunlight. It was only an illusion, which faded when he shook his head, but somehow it seemed far more real, as if somehow he had been able to leave the Sevilla slums and approach a distant plane, where he stood as a silent, unseen observer, studying another man who stood in the midst of a forsaken bullring.

Waiting? Waiting for what? He never gave himself time to answer, going through the door, where a short, stumpy man of about sixty greeted him. The old man looked up and said something in Spanish, but when he saw the intruder was not a native, he experimented, first in French, then German, and finally hitting it right with English.

"You are British? No, American? What can I do to help you?"

"I think you should speak your own language," Catron answered, continuing the conversation in Spanish for the listener's benefit. "I have only one thing to ask you about."

"Then ask," the old man responded, extending his hands in an expression of simplicity, like the famous statue of Christ so often reproduced on calendars and paintings.

"If you are Paco Solorzano, that is. If so, I have only one thing to ask about. I'm a writer, and I'll pay you for your time."

The old man's eyes narrowed in sudden suspicion, but he nodded in the affirmative. He was Solorzano, the man who had been at Jaime Sublaran's side for so long, who had been in Huelva, taking movies. With the nod of recognition, Catron continued. He spoke only two words when he was cut off.

"Jaime Sublaran . . ."

"Come back some other time and we'll talk about it," the old man stuttered, ushering him out with amazing swiftness for someone so elderly and mild looking. "Maybe a hundred years from now!"

Catron found himself in the street, the door shut and locked behind him. Strange that after over twenty years the very mentioning of the name would cause such a panic in a man who had once known him so well. An odd reaction, but one which fired his writer's curiosity, prompting him, rather than dampening, forcing him to continue in his search for pieces to the puzzle. There was something in the background about Jaime Sublaran, something which made all those connected with him uncomfortable, as if he had not once been a living, breathing man, but a nightmare, vanishing with the break of daylight and the ringing of an alarm clock.

That night, Catron checked into a hotel room close to Solorzano's workshop, moving to an area which better fitted his needs. He did not bother to call back in Huelva, as he'd promised to do each night. He was sick of them nursing him, treating him like some kind of psychopath who belonged in a rubber cell, talking to himself and to the padded walls. Instead, he plotted in bed, drawing up plans for another approach toward Solorzano, finding out what he wanted to learn, and devising alternatives if he could not. When he finally went to sleep, he dreamed once again of the matador in gold and black, knowing somehow that though he didn't see the face, it belonged to Jaime Sublaran.

He did call home the following morning, leaving a message that he'd be back within three days. If he didn't have what he wanted by then, he decided it was pretty much out of reach to begin with. From lunchtime until twilight, he lingered outside the area surrounding the sword shop, waiting for Solorzano to finally close. When the moment came, he followed the diminutive old man at a distance, down the side streets to a small saloon. He hung around outside for a short time so as not to look too suspicious, before going in. When he finally did enter, he saw the situation was ideal.

Aside from the owner, Solorzano was the only man in the bar, and he was fast approaching drunkenness. Calmly, he approached the sword-maker's table and asked if the face rang a bell. Solorzano failed to understand the American expression, so the author repeated himself, using Spanish terminology. The old man's eyes widened momentarily, but the uneasiness vanished as quickly as it materialized and he motioned Catron to take a seat.

"Two more wines," he said to the waiter, taking a cigarette from his package of Celtas without offering one to Catron, who didn't really care. He hadn't smoked in three years and besides, that wasn't the purpose of his confrontation. He wanted to know about Sublaran and why there was so much secrecy involving him. He didn't have to ask twice, for the old man sensed what was coming, like a rat smelling the cheese that baited a trap.

"I have never known peace since that day, when Jaime Sublaran died. It doesn't happen often anymore. Once or twice every five years someone comes, wanting to hear the story. Well, the story has been told. It doesn't need telling again. Some things are better left dead!"

"I know the story," Catron replied, ordering another drink in reserve for the old man. With enough poured into him, he'd loosen up. "I don't want to know the gossip or the rumors or anything about the death of Jaime Sublaran. I want to know what he was like when he was alive."

Solorzano's lips narrowed and the wrinkles in his face stood out more, like the few remaining strands of hair on his head, the picture of in-depth thought. He considered his answer carefully, then the words came from his lips, as slow and calculating as a perfectly delivered sword thrust.

"Sublaran was a matador! There is no other word! He was a . . . matador! He fit the image like no other man."

"What do you mean?"

Hungry now, Catron was probing him further. The mouse was taking the bait, reverting back to the scene in Huelva, where Cristo Cruz ended his life.

"You know, you could see the bullets going through his head. The blood shot out, with little pieces of skull and brains. It all flew into the air, quick, but you could see it happening. He blew his whole head off, in front of everybody."

Solorzano put his hands on top his bald head, pointing his fingers upward, wiggling them in a poor imitation of flying blood.

"Like this. Zip! Zip! Zip! Zip! Zip! He put a whole bunch of holes in his head. The top of it looked like Swiss cheese. When they took him to the infirmary, someone had to follow behind, with his hands on Cristo Cruz's head. They were holding the top of his skull on so it wouldn't fall off."

Solorzano stopped dead and burped, making no effort to control himself. The memories were not ones he cared to remember. No one, except perhaps Jaime Sublaran himself, who seemed more depraved and deranged by the minute, could have cherished such thoughts or been considered lucky to have viewed the spectacle as it happened.

"And they still think I'm losing my mind," Catron mused silently, thinking of his clan back in Huelva, rooming in a house once owned by perhaps the greatest lunatic the world of bullfighting had ever known. "They think I'm having a nervous breakdown because my hands shake and my stomach bothers me. Christ, what would they do if I went to a bullfight with a movie camera and started yelling for the matador to grab a submachine gun and blow his brains out so I could get it on film like Jaime Sublaran? Now there's a nut, man, a nut . . . but one worth money. I can smell it like fresh cut grass."

The old man was in another world, one long dead, but brought to life again, both out of drunkenness and a memory rekindled by the questions, leaving him to relive the past, there in a Sevilla bar, long after the incidents had passed into history. A series of short, strange noises escaped from his lips, as he closed his eyes, trying to focus on a thought he'd long since sought to banish from his mind, knowing all the while that to do so was impossible. Finished, he remained silent, then again, the unnatural spurts leaked out. It was a poorly done imitation of a bullring band, playing the opening notes to "La Ultima Estocada," the Sublaran theme.

Catron waited, sipping on his own wine, for the old man had withdrawn from his dreamworld. When he did, he seemed like a changed man, more open, more confident.

"He was the matador supreme. He had style, Mister American. It was always the same. A ritual. Sublaran's life was a series of rituals, both in and out of the ring."

Catron gestured with his hands for Solorzano to continue, all the while nudging the second wine glass toward him, wanting him to drink more. It was working, moving more smoothly than he'd hoped for.

"Sublaran would stand far off from the bull, the sword and the *muleta*, the little red lure, in his right hand, his left hand empty.

Then he would motion, point up into the stands, signaling for the bullring band, letting them know it was time for 'La Ultima Estocada.' This was his song, his theme, his background music. You've heard it, haven't you? It begins with a trumpet solo, then the whole band plays, marchlike. There is danger in the song, my friend, in every note, putting suspense in the air. Sublaran knew that and capitalized because of it, blending the melody with his performance.''

Catron sipped his wine, picturing the matador in his mind once more, dressed in black and gold, in the center of an unidentified bullring, only this time with a live bull. Yet as he thought, the old man was still talking. He shook his head, bringing himself back to reality. He couldn't lose track of what was being said. This was once-in-a-lifetime material.

"The band would always have to play 'La Ultima Estocada,' '' Solorzano went on. "If they didn't know it, Sublaran would bring the musical score and have it sent to them before the fight. That's when he'd begin, when they were playing his song. He called it his "cat walk." Like a man on a highwire, dancing fifty feet above the ground without a net. That's what it was like. He would pose, motionless, as the trumpet solo began, preparing himself, then, in time to the first crash of notes, when the whole band played together, he'd take a step toward the bull . . . then another . . . and another . . . like ballet . . . a dance with death. Closer and closer he'd come, approaching the bull, coming to it rather than it coming to him, daring it to kill him. By God, it was like he believed himself protected, above the clutches of a goring, with a secret power behind him no one else could see. That's how he always did it, walking toward the bull, slowly, ritualistic, moving closer with each step, toward death on the horns. Finally the bull would charge. That's when he'd stop walking, his feet nailed to the ground, and he'd start his series of passes with the animal. He'd link pass after pass, again and again. The bull would always obey his wishes, as if he'd cast a spell upon it or sprinkled some sort of magic powder on the cape, so the bull would follow it no matter what.''

The old man paused, finishing the second glass of wine. He was sweating, his eyes growing glassy, his accented speech now somewhat slurred. Catron ordered him another drink and probed him onward.

"How interesting. Now what about his private life? There are a lot of rumors."

Solorzano hesitated, as if once again fear had gripped his throat, strangling him, preventing the words from escaping, but they did. Slowly, confusingly, they came, the truth about Jaime Sublaran from one of the few men who knew him well.

"Sublaran couldn't have been buried in the traditional way, even if he wanted to. He was excommunicated because he was involved in a lot of strange things that were covered up until the time he died. He'd go to see the *brujas*, the witches and the fortune tellers in Sevilla and Huelva. Once I even had to go with him to Ireland to attend some sort of stupid ritual. A Black Mass or something, the ceremony of some crazy cult. Druid-oriented, I remember it described. Sublaran greatly enjoyed the abnormal. Me, I went along out of curiosity, though my presence was not particularly welcomed among the group. I didn't like it. I saw what the activities were doing to his mind. The pressures of being a top matador, mixed with his personal conflicts and all this crazy stuff he kept seeing and reading, reduced him to a complete wreck. His nerves were showing those final seasons, particularly after the Cristo Cruz incident. When Jaime died, there were plenty of ill omens."

"What do you mean?" Catron questioned, ordering yet another wine, though Solorzano mildly protested. "You've got to do better than that."

"For one thing, Jaime Sublaran never went into the chapel at the bullring to pray, Mister American. After all, he was excommunicated. For what, I don't know. I heard it was because of a scandal he caused in Mexico. He got this nun pregnant and she left the church, but when he refused to marry her, she committed suicide—found dead with a gun in one hand and a picture of him in the other. That isn't the point. The point is he scorned Christianity, the Catholics in particular. He had no religion that I know of, though outwardly he bordered on satanic. Yet that day in Madrid, he went into the chapel to pray."

An unnatural silence came as Solorzano restudied his statements and Catron listened. Then the old man continued, having considered things more carefully, realizing that though he was drunk, his statements were indeed accurate.

"I think he finally lost his faith in himself or whatever he believed in and tried to turn back to the old beliefs. I think perhaps God was offended, profaned by what happened, and that's why he was killed."

The old man caught the smirk Catron was desperately trying to hold back and exploded, growing calm once the words were out.

"Either God was offended because Sublaran prayed to him . . . or the devil was angered because Sublaran no longer held faith in himself or the crazy things he was involved in, because that day nothing went right. From the early morning on, there were omens."

"Now what do you mean?" Catron asked again, growing tired of having to repeat himself, but enduring. First, it was great background for his book. Second, it was fascinating. Like the late matador, he too was interested in the uncanny.

"Sublaran had nightmares all week," Solorzano continued, growing increasingly nervous. It showed. He was pecking at the table with his fingers, wanting another cigarette, but holding back. "He dreamed he was in an empty bullring, dressed in his favorite suit of black and gold, the one he was wearing the day he was killed. He dreamed that there, with row after row of empty seats staring down at him, Cristo Cruz reached up from the ground, a rotting, half-skeletal corpse, still dressed in a matador's costume of his own, rising to grab him, pulling him down into the earth, into the grave, and into hell to join him. At long last I think Sublaran was feeling guilty about the incident, though you wouldn't have thought it that day in Huelva. He was happy then, God forgive us both. Happy. He was laughing!"

A chill shot through Catron as he thought of his own daydream, the one that had been cropping up in his mind since he arrived in Sevilla, of the matador standing alone in an empty bullring, dressed in black and gold. Only now he knew who he was and what he was waiting for. He was Jaime Sublaran and he was waiting for death!

"Maybe there's more to the supernatural than we'll ever know," Catron said, swallowing uneasily, longing to smoke for the first time in over a year. "The flesh is dead, but the spirit lives on, right?

So continue. This is getting good."

The old man took one of his Celtas, offering to share the pack, but he was turned down. It took Solorzano several tries to finally light it successfully. His hands were shaking, not just out of drunken clumsiness, but of something else, unexplainable, a cold, unseen fear, invisible to the eye, but felt by the rest of the senses.

"The ranch number branded on the flank of the bull that killed him was thirty-five. In Madrid, the number on Sublaran's hotel room door was number thirty-five, and the first two numbers on his automobile license plates were thirty-five. When we drove to the arena, we had a flat tire halfway there. Sublaran and his helpers had to get out and take a taxi. It was as if some force was trying to keep him from going to the bullring, keeping him from meeting destiny. Sublaran sensed it too. I told you, he was so unnerved, he even went into the chapel to pray."

Catron was devouring every word. He didn't need to write it down. He'd remember it all. It was one of his talents.

"The name of the bull that killed him was El Diablo, as big and as difficult as the last animal Cristo Cruz fought in Huelva, the one he failed so badly with. Do you know what else, my friend? No, of course you don't, but I'll tell you. The day Sublaran died on the horns was also an anniversary. It was Cristo Cruz's birthdate. You see, Mister American, there are omens that never leave us. The only problem is we never see the signs in time."

"Yes, Señor Solorzano, I'm beginning to see. Do you have any more to tell me? Anything? The goring? The trip to Ireland? This change over the years that happened to Sublaran? What took place in Huelva when Cristo Cruz decided to shoot himself?"

"Huelva was a nightmare come true," the old man stuttered at the memory. "I took movies of all of Jaime's fights. He kept them in his home, on file. As far as I know , that's where you'd find them, but how you'd get hold of whoever's crazy enough to be living in Sublaran's house now, I don't know."

Catron bit back a smile as he tasted his wine. What the old man didn't know wouldn't hurt him. Just like the cliche he'd always hated, but had seen proven true. It was a key to success when probing someone for information.

"Anyway, American, I was taking movies of my matador in Huelva, just like always," the old man went on, sweat now covering his face and hands, more obviously than ever, making his bald head shine against the light of the bar. "I didn't take any movies of Cruz. Sublaran didn't want movies of anyone but himself, but then he changed all of a sudden. Cristo Cruz was having a tantrum, crying in shame and disgrace. Sublaran told me to take a picture of it and I did, a quick one, figuring he found it funny and wanted to remember it. After all, he had a strange sense of humor. I took the shot then put the camera down, but Sublaran was furious. He told me to keep filming, not stopping until I was told. It shocked me! It wasn't like him! It broke the pattern, but I listened to him. Now I think back and realize it was like he knew somehow what was going to happen next, when Cristo Cruz grabbed that gun and pumped those machine gun bullets into his head. So help me, I got it all on film. You could see the holes being made, where the bullets went in and out. God help me, I filmed it all . . . and as I did, that madman was laughing!"

"Laughing?" Catron's eyebrows raised. "Is that when the picture was taken, the one that appeared in all the magazines?"

Solorzano nodded, finishing off his wine and ordering a round on his own. Catron didn't want it. His stomach was bothering him, the dull pains already coming back, but he forced himself. Instinct told him there was a little more to go.

"I'll tell you, Mister American, I, Paco Solorzano, was once the right hand man to Jaime Sublaran, and even I feared him during those last few years. He wasn't normal anymore. He was sick. I knew it long before the magazine photo came out. All that did was make his sickness obvious to everyone else, confirming what I already knew. Yet I stuck by him, right until the end."

Solorzano paused, taking another gulp of wine before going on, now all but lost to reality.

"I saw it when Cristo Cruz died, and I saw it when the horn found Jaime Sublaran. Neither time was pretty, nothing you'd want to see before going out to dinner. I saw it when Sublaran was killed. The air was full of bad omens . . . "

Solorzano was repeating himself and the writer sought to change the subject before the wine overtook him entirely, bringing an end to all valid conversation. "What about Cristo Cruz? Could he have really rivaled Jaime Sublaran as a matador?"

The old man thought for a moment, then answered, going for yet another Celta as he spoke.

"There was something wrong with Cristo Cruz in Huelva that day. It was like a contest, not just Cruz against Jaime Sublaran, but god against god, the Catholic Lord of Cruz pitted against whatever it was Sublaran believed in . . . and exactly what that was . . . I'm not sure. That day in Huelva, the god of Jaime Sublaran prevailed. In Madrid, the god of the Catholics took his long-awaited revenge and struck back. I told that to the press once. They laughed at me, said I was just adding on to the superstition. God knows, there's been enough superstition and rumor involving Jaime Sublaran. You know, people say his ghost haunts his home in Huelva and the bullring there, that his spirit has been seen in Madrid's Ventas bullring and walking the streets of Sevilla."

"He's awful busy for one ghost then," Catron joked, before realizing he'd made his last mistake. The old man jumped up from the table, pounding his fists downward, lurching as his wine-drugged mind tried to control his body from a thousand miles away.

"Mister American, you insult me," the old man babbled. "I saw that goring and still have nightmares about it. He was gored under the jaw! The horn all but tore his head off! The tip gouged out his eye from the inside! Why do you think the papers edited the photos? The bull kept hooking into his face, again and again, destroying him. I vomited when it happened and so did half of the people in the bullring."

Solorzano turned, stumbling against the wall, then started forward, his arms swaying back and forth, like a child imitating a steam locomotive, trying to maintain his balance as he made his way off into the night. From the table, Phil Catron watched him go, making no effort to stop him, knowing full well he'd already milked him dry and there was little more to be learned from the retired manager-turned-drunken-sword maker . . . at least as far as the man wanted to tell.

Leaning back, he thought once again of the picture which had flesh is dead, but the spirit lives on.''

Just another silly sentence going through his mind as he tried
of something to write on paper. But the sound. It had been
low murmur, made loud only because fifteen thousand
had muttered it at once.

murmur before the cheers.''

st have been like that always, just before Jaime Sublaran
s famous Cat Walk. Profiling, far away from the bull, the
stiffened, his back arched, head tilted back, cape and sword
ont of him, in his right hand. As he shook the cloth, the
rose, signaling the band, letting them know it was time
hen, at that moment, between the silence and the cheers,
ring band started to play, came the murmur, escaping from
of every fan. They knew what was coming next. It was
aran was giving them what they had paid to see.

ltima Estocada''—Catron had heard it before. The open-
lonely trumpet solo, then the entire band started to play
a marchlike pattern to match the matador's footsteps as
his way toward possible death on the golden sand.

and would always have to play 'La Ultima Estocada.' ''
turned toward the old monograph record player and the
d, questions which he had somehow ignored immediately
to his mind.

years before, Jaime Sublaran used this very study and
. There for his comfort? He must have played them in
of his private quarters. The melodies must have re-
made him forget who he was and how he made his liv-
adn't he even bothered to look inside the stand, to see
here? Even if the record player didn't work and the
scratched beyond repair, there still might have been
orth seeing that would have left another clue involving
and his personal tastes. What kind of music did he like,
La Ultima Estocada?'' There was only one way to find

aped toward the record stand, only to be shot down
ned the door and found just three records within the
ing out the albums, he didn't have to read the titles to

been cropping up in his mind, of the mysterious matador in black
and gold, waiting alone in the empty plaza for death to strike or
the late Cristo Cruz to rise out of the open mouth of hell to claim
the one who had indirectly pressed him to suicide and laughed
hilariously about it afterward. The vision lingered for a little while,
then faded, replaced by another thought, even more disappointing.

Phil Catron, American author on the verge of a nervous
breakdown, had been all but dragged protestingly to southern Spain,
kicking and screaming all the way, by family and friends, to pull
him away from his work, only to place him in a situation where
he'd wound up landing in the midst of a situation they'd tried forcing
him to avoid. To make matters worse, Jaime Sublaran, the proposed
subject of his next book, was still little more than a dark and
brooding character from the past. Though much of the mystery
about the man had been uncovered in the conversation with Paco
Solorzano, new, even more troublesome questions had materialized
in place of those which had been answered.

The late Jaime Sublaran, be he vindictive madman, talented
matador, devil worshiper, or the simple product of distorted gossip,
was as much an enigma to him now as when he'd first heard the
name.

# 5

# FIXATION

Catron alone in the silence of the massive study, sat behind the desk that had once been used by Jaime Sublaran. In front of him, the typewriter remained inactive, only a few words pecked across the inserted page. While his research into the personal life of the controversial matador had thus far been successful, the writing part of the program was moving along far too slowly. No matter how hard he tried, he couldn't keep his mind from drifting off the manuscript toward the brooding portrait that hung directly across from him. Clearly, his imagination was working overtime, for whenever he did start to put a sentence together, he found himself stopping midway, raising his eyes up to the painting, as if he expected to find it changed, like in Wilde's book about Dorian Grey, or gone entirely, come to life and creeping toward him.

"He always made Solorzano take movies."

Catron turned his attention to the pile of films on his desk, four 200-foot metal reels of old standard 8mm home movies. Later, when nightfall came, he planned a showing, not only for himself but for the entire family. They hadn't been hard to find. Not at all. The first closet he'd opened upon returning from Sevilla had proven successful, revealing not only two stacks of encased movie film, over three feet high from base to top, but an old projector and movie screen as well. Obviously, his luck was changing. Fate had intervened again, guiding him toward each new find as he unwound the mystery behind Jaime Sublaran and prepared to put what he discovered into print.

Next to the films on the desk were so
books, printed years before Sublaran's
death. The authors, writing in Spanish
Huelva as the newest revelation in the
tioned pictures of their hero in actic
Though he had done so at least a doze
to leaf through the pages, studying at a
convincing the crowd he was in fact th

"Strange," he thought, consider
books and magazines about him whe
nothing about his private life or what
all seem afraid. They don't want to

Such knowledge suited him fine
would be the first and thus bring

"The Cat Walk."

One of the pictures showed Sub
the camera. In the foreground, the s
of a bull were definite. As he looke
see one foot in front of the othe
matador in freeze frame, steppin
leaving no doubts whatsoever cor

"He called it his Cat Walk .

He could hear the crowd, not
of nervous anticipation, rising up
of the bullring band as the mata

"The band would always pla

Catron lifted his eyes from
painting, as if responding to a
locked with the cold-hearted ex
down with unseeing, oil-painted

Catron winced, the words go
"Heaven and Earth. Heaven a
an illusion? The mind is its ov

He closed the book and to
typing, but he'd hit only a doze
caused him to bolt from the cl
again nailing upon the portra

"Th
No.
to think
there,
tongues

"Th
It m
started h
matador
held in
left hand
to start.
as the bu
the throa
time. Su

"La l
ing was a
together,
he inched

"The
Catron
record sta
popping i

Twenty
the record
the solitud
laxed him,
ing. Why
what was
records we
something
the matado
aside from
out.

Catron
when he op
cabinet. Pu

realize they were recordings of bullfight songs, for each one had a photograph or reproduction of a matador and a bull on the cover. The titles on the back were much the same, though played by different bands in each case. "El Gato Montez," "Espana Cani," "Nino de La Palma," "Gallito." Music of the bullring, without variation, yet each album had another common denominator, which was not completely unpredictable. All three recordings contained a version of "La Ultima Estocada."

"His song. This was his song."

Catron plugged the cord into the socket and flicked the switch, relieved when the turntable started to play. The record player worked and the needle, once plucked free from a huge ball of dust, seemed to be in suitable condition.

"He was the matador supreme."

As the needle made contact, the record made a series of short, static pops, then silence, followed by the lonely wail of a trumpet, far off in the distance. As the song progressed, the brass instrument seemed to grow louder, closer, then the entire room was filled with the crashing notes of "La Ultima Estocada" in full swing, the band playing together, blending the lone trumpeter's mournful lament with all the electricity and excitement of an actual bullfight.

Catron closed his eyes, picturing how it must have been. Sublaran, dark and defiant, a smirk on his face as he studied the bull from afar, then gingerly placing one foot in front of the other, starting his advance while the crowd roared with approval.

"He called it his Cat Walk."

Bull and man met at midring, Sublaran flicking the cape outward, to divert the animal's attack. Again he did it, and again, leading the bull in circles around his waist.

"Like ballet . . . "

The bull was hypnotized by the dancing lure, controlled by the man who manipulated it. The brassy notes of "La Ultima Estocada" were all but drowned out by the screams and cheers of the crowd as Sublaran worked his magic, dominating his horned adversary, making it obey every command he issued.

"He was the matador supreme."

The bull charged when Sublaran told it to charge, stopped when he told it to stop. As he finished his final series, he dropped to his knees, casting the cape aside to expose himself unarmed before the animal. He had convinced the crowd, down to the most embittered critic, that he was indeed the master matador.

"His courage knew no limits. He was the matador supreme, the maestro of all maestros. At times he fought like a man possessed by a hundred demons from hell."

The matador rose, gathering up his cape and sword, walking away, his back to the tired beast as if it weren't even there. First came the cheers, then the chant, growing louder each time it was repeated.

"Sublaran! Sublaran! Sublaran! Sublaran! Sublaran!"

With the mingling of kettledrums and brass, the final notes of "La Ultima Estocada" carried the figure away, leaving Catron awake, shaking his head.

"The flesh is dead, but the spirit lives on."

For a moment there was silence, then another song off the record filled the air. Catron didn't recognize it, didn't like it. Reaching forward, he plucked up the phonograph's arm, hearing the scratch of needle against record as he placed it back at the original starting point. Again came the popping and crackling, then finally the opening trumpet call of "La Ultima Estocada."

Sublaran's theme. It was a nice song. As the melody progressed, Catron found himself uncontrollably reaching for the volume knob, cranking it up so the music boomed with the full-scale effect of a bullfight in progress. Only this time he did not close his eyes nor allow himself to dream of the dancing figure in black and gold, drifting instead toward the painting of the matador.

"The flesh is dead, but the spirit lives on."

No matter how hard he tried, he could not shake the sentence from his mind. A ludicrous statement . . . but what if it were true? From somewhere in a world invisible to the human eye, but nonetheless real, perhaps the restless spirit of the unfortunate matador did survive, maybe in the corridors of his own house, waiting all these years for someone like Catron to come along, someone who could write his story, the true story, apart from all the slander and gossip, clearing the name of Jaime Sublaran.

"It was like a contest, not just Cruz against Jaime Sublaran, but god against god . . ."

"If only Paco Solorzano had known," said Catron to himself. "The poor, half-mad, drunken fool had spent much of his life with Sublaran, yet he didn't know him, didn't understand him, didn't try to get past his own biases and to the root of things."

Sublaran didn't deserve the slander and the hatred. If anything, he was a pathetic man, clinging desperately to his role as the greatest matador of all time, unable to cope with anyone or anything intent on taking that position from him. The matador deserved sympathy. Yes, sympathy, an effort to understand what was really going on in his mind.

"Bullfighter," Catron grumbled aloud. "Greatest of all time. Idol with no rival."

As the music boomed, he approached the painting, looking up to zero in on the matador's features. There was no real hatred in the face, not as he'd first noticed it, but an embittered hurt, much like Christ as depicted on the cross. The eyes no longer blazed with hellish flames, but contained a sadness, unable to mask the heart-break Sublaran must have felt when the public turned on him.

"Greatest of all time," Catron repeated. "No rival."

From the eyes he could see tears, literally, running down the painted cheeks, wet and flowing. Crying! The painting was crying, like the alleged miracles he read about in gossip papers, about the crying madonnas and patron saints that wept for the sinful condition of the world.

"Matador."

He halfway expected the tears to turn to blood, bright and crimson, tainted like his reputation. Those bastards in the stands. The many-headed monster. It was Manolete, another great matador who had known the agony of having his fans turn on him, the same as Sublaran, that first called the public a monster. How true his statement had proven to be, time and time again.

"The people in the stands combine to make a single, living unit, a many-headed monster that drools in hungry anticipation, eager to see a top matador fall once he reaches the top. Having made a man an idol, the monster takes no greater delight than to see that idol crumble, through disgrace or death with the rip of a horn into flesh."

"La Ultima Estocada" was reaching its climax for the second

time, the frenzied playing of the band serving as indication that the end was near. Yet, as the melody played, the face of Jaime Sublaran came alive, the lips parting in preparation to speak. Amid the trumpets and the woodwinds was the roar of the crowd, only this time they weren't cheering, they were booing.

Catron closed his eyes, placed his hands to his ears, trying to drown out the noise, but it did no good. When he gave in to the mass hysteria of the unseen yet very audible crowd he saw what he had feared the most. The tears which had streamed watery white now glistened in shining scarlet. The tears had turned to blood.

"Jesus Christ," came a voice from behind, "do you have to play that damned music so loud? What the hell are you trying to do, cave the house in!"

Catron turned around, but the room was spinning, whirling about him in a mass of flying colors. The sounds of "La Ultima Estocada" swarmed in circles around his head, separating him from the real world. Then, as suddenly as it started, it had stopped.

"What the hell is wrong with you!"

Dennis Flagstaff had shut off the record player and was looking directly at him, his face a mask of disgust. Had the faces of the fans been like that when they turned on Jaime Sublaran? Catron wondered about this, but he was given no time to speak.

"Man, you're working too hard again. You'd better watch yourself."

Catron sighed deeply, walking past his brother-in-law and sitting at the desk, as if to resume typing. Dennis wasn't fooled. He pulled the paper out of the machine and dropped it on the floor. His eyes were as serious as those of the matador in the painting.

"Man, you're pressing it again. That trip to Sevilla, the films, now the goddamned music. You're going to overdose on this Sublaran idea, Phil. This thing you're doing isn't good. Your ulcer's going to act up, and you'll be puking from now until we leave."

"I can take care of myself," Catron snorted, bending over to pick up the piece of typing paper. As he leaned forward, he felt for the first time the drops of moisture on his forehead. As he brought up his free hand to wipe himself he realized it was soaked.

"I'm not pressing," he said, but stammered on the words, a telltale sign he prayed would not manifest. "I just got caught up in the music. It's how I work."

"It's how you'll get a nervous breakdown or give the rest of us one," Flagstaff retorted sharply, leaning over the desk, his face almost level with Catron's. "You were brought to Spain to relax. I paid the tab, remember. You can do this shit at home and crack up on your own time and money, but I'll be damned if you'll do it on mine."

Catron took a deep breath and blinked repeatedly. Sweat was getting in his eyes. It was starting to burn.

"I'll be all right," he said at long last, though his brother-in-law seemed scarcely convinced. "We have movie time tonight, then Freddie and I have the bullfight to go to in a couple days while you and my sister are gone. I have plenty of time to relax. We all do."

Dennis reached forward as if to knock the reels of movie film to the floor, but Catron caught his wrist, holding it steady.

"That wouldn't be a wise thing to do," he said, still clamping on. "I said I'll be all right . . . if you get your ass out of here and let me do my work. You're a wrestler, not a writer. You use your body, not your brain. No way in hell will you be able to understand all this or appreciate what I'm doing."

"Well, I have something for you to understand," Dennis hissed, his voice sounding half-human and half-gila monster. "It's about that guy you went to see in Sevilla. The one you were bragging about, giving you the story of a lifetime. Solorzano? Right? Paco Solorzano. The guy connected with Jaime Sublaran."

"Speak."

"Someone spoke to him all right and more. It's in the paper. He was found dead, been that way for days, with his throat cut."

Catron's face didn't reflect the slightest bit of sorrow or compassion, only a mild flinch of surprise. It took him a few seconds to form the words and when they came, Dennis was startled.

"He was alive and kicking when I was in Sevilla last week. Do they know who snuffed out his candle?"

"It doesn't bother you? It would give me the creeps."

"Why should it bother me?" Catron shrugged. He was still holding Flagstaff's wrist. The grip was tightening.

"You were all keyed up about talking to him. You said he'd given you the background for this new book project of yours. You acted like you'd met Jesus Christ out there."

"I talked to him, Dennis. I didn't say I knew him, for God's sake. Besides, with him out of the way like this, it'll make even better reading. I can add another chapter about it in the manuscript. By chance did you bring the newspaper with you? I'd like to see the article about him."

Flagstaff tried to recoil, shocked at his brother-in-law's obvious indifference, but he couldn't get away from the grip. Though he had previously thought himself at least three times as strong as Phil Catron, he couldn't break free of the grip. He seemed to have a new strength, coming from some hidden source.

"You mean it doesn't bother you?"

"Mister, it doesn't bother me in the slightest. My heart pumps piss for him, through paper arteries! In fact, I'm glad it happened. It'll help increase sales."

"Let go of me, you son of a bitch," Dennis ordered in a voice more authoritative than he'd first intended it.

"My grip is loose, hotshot," Catron said coolly, masking a snicker, which was not his typical type of laugh. "All you've got to do is yank yourself away, or aren't you the big, bad pro-wrestler you're always claiming to be? When you're out here and your fights aren't rigged, you aren't so tough, are you, baby?"

"Go to hell, brother-in-law!"

"Sure thing, champ. When I'm down there, I'll say hello to all your friends and relatives. Now let me get back to work and you can go practice your fake expressions in front of the mirror, for next time some wrestler puts you in an armlock, okay? Just stay the hell out of my business . . . and my life!"

"Wrestling's all real!" Flagstaff retorted angrily.

Catron's grip tightened again on his relative's wrist. A fight was brewing.

"Real, you ass! Wrestling hasn't been real since the days of Gorgeous George. You're just a phoney and the only reason you got to marry my sister was because she was stupid enough to believe you were something special because of all that bullshit you do in the ring! It's not surprising she'd fall for someone like you, though.

She was nothing but a slut to begin with, ever since we were growing up.''

Flagstaff's face was livid. Either way, win or lose, he knew he'd come out on the short end. He could hit his brother-in-law and have his wife mad at both of them, or he could ignore the remarks and look like an absolute asshole. Instead, he tried his best to compromise.

"Phil, I know you get moody and irrational at times, but I should beat the shit out of you for saying stuff about my wife like that!''

Catron smiled pleasantly, his grip relaxing somewhat. "You should get a V.D. shot. That's what you should do, hero, after sleeping with that slut!''

Exasperated, Dennis pulled his wrist free and stormed from the room, mumbling curses under his breath. Catron watched him go, then slowly hit a few keys on the typewriter. When he finished, he'd only created two words:

"Jaime Sublaran.''

As he read them aloud, he looked back at the picture, knowing full well there would be no movement, no tears, no crying of blood.

"The spirit lives on.''

Was he actually beginning to believe that? No. It was just his own mind being overworked, obsessed with a powerful character, fact stranger than fiction, more baffling than any imagined character he had ever dreamed up over a cup of coffee or winter night's sleep, to put in a novel. This man was truly a demon, but the devil always was more colorful than God, evil more sought after than good.

"The spirit lives. Yes, it does live on!''

Catron continued to type, working hard until he completed a whole paragraph, the words coming naturally, flowing from his brain into his fingers. Proudly, he read his finished piece of work, not caring if anyone heard, mortal or ghost.

"Jaime Sublaran was an absolute enigma, misunderstood by his church, his fans, his countrymen, and his fellow bullfighters. He was, however, the greatest matador in the history of the art form, a proven fact that none of the efforts to slander his name will ever be able to take away.''

Stifling a chuckle, Catron again raised his head toward the picture and cast an uneasy smile.

"You approve?'' he asked the painting.

As could be expected, no answer came.

# 6

# DEATH IN THE ARENA

Nightfall had come to Huelva. As the others waited in the massive den, Catron prepared the first of the films to be shown. He'd set the projector on top the desk, adjusting the screen on the opposite side of the room near the big oil painting. In a distorted semicircle, he'd arranged three chairs, the desk chair for himself, the rest for his companions. Freddie and Dennis fidgeted in their seats, the latter not really anxious to see the exhibition, while Patsy sat by the lights, waiting for the signal to shut them off.

As the film's leader clicked through the camera, Catron was talking to himself, but no one else heard his words. They were garbled praised of Jaime Sublaran's ability and how unjust the public had been when they turned on him. "Okay," he said, as he slipped the first bit of film into the notch in the takeup reel. "Let's get the show rolling."

Patsy hit the switch, encasing the room in total darkness. She had a difficult time making it to her seat but Catron waited before flipping the projector light on and starting the film forward. Instantly, an image flashed across the screen quite distinguishable as an interior shot of the Huelva bullring, though the print was scratched and splotted with black dots.

Catron eased himself into the desk chair and settled down, though he seemed to be the only one enjoying the movie. On the screen he watched as the matadors, followed by their assistants, the banderilleros, and picadors, made their way across the ring in the

46

traditional opening parade. No one had to tell him that the man in the black and gold costume was Jaime Sublaran and the song the band must have been playing that afternoon was "La Ultima Estocada."

"Paco Solorzano was killed."

Catron shut his eyes. On the screen the others watched as a huge bull darted into the ring, circling the sand in search of something to kill. Suddenly, the man in black and gold darted out from the protective barrier and dropped to his knees on the ground, the cape furled out in front of him. The bull turned to see the kneeling man and started toward him. The matador, however, showed no fear, waiting, letting the animal bear down on him, then just when its horns seemed to reach his face, he flipped the cape upward, over his shoulder and the beast thundered by him, passing so closely the horntip knocked the bullfighter's cap off his head.

"Jesus!" Freddie said. He was the only one in the small group who had any comment. "That was Sublaran, right? He really was as crazy as the legends have him."

Crazy! The word flared up like fire from a blowtorch in Catron's mind. Crazy! Another defamer. Everyone knocked Sublaran. How quickly they forgot his ability in the ring. Crazy? No, Sublaran wasn't crazy. The rest of the world was mad.

"Jesus," Freddie repeated, "he's doing it again!"

Sublaran spun on his kneecaps to reposition himself, receiving the bull with an identical pass on the opposite side, accepting the bull's return charge. Again he did it, then again, rising for another series of passes on his feet, before turning to walk away. The animal was under his spell, like all of them, doing his bidding.

"The bull would always obey his wishes, as if he'd cast a spell upon it or sprinkled some sort of magic powder on the cape, so the bull would follow it, no matter what . . . "

Catron had opened his eyes. He was watching the screen as the mounted picadors came in on their horses, prodding the bull's shoulders with their spear-tipped poles. Their purpose was to weaken the animal's shoulder muscles so the beast would be forced to lower its head and slow down its charge. It was mandatory, for if the animal remained as it did when first entering the ring, coming hard and strong, with head held high, it would be impossible for the matador to make his closer, more elegant capework later on, or drive the sword into the correct spot, the gap between the bull's shoulder blades that opens only when the head is low, making a successful kill.

Afterward, the banderilleros came in and placed the banderillas, the 2½-foot, paper-covered shafts of wood, with pronglike tips, in the back of the animal, serving the same general purpose as the picador's spear, only executed with a greater degree of nobility and therefore more favorably received by the crowd. The banderillas were always placed in three sets of pairs. Sublaran often placed his own, rather than relying on his hired help, winning more applause by his actions and adding to his prowess as a master bullfighter. On occasion, he would even snap the banderilla shafts in half before putting them in, reducing them to a mere six inches and tripling the risks of a goring.

"Paco Solorzano is dead."

"How fitting," Catron told himself. "Solorzano was just like all the others, all of those who . . . "

His eyes left the screen, raising up to the oil painting, which was barely visible in the darkness. He continued his conversation under his breath, as if talking to the portrait.

"They all double-crossed you. All of them. Even though they pushed you to your death, you still live on. They have tried to forget you, but they will never bury you. When my book is finished, they're all going to know, all going to understand."

On the screen, Sublaran had the cape and sword, starting his famous Cat Walk toward the bull. Freddie and Dennis were interested, but Patsy was bored, yawning.

Sublaran dropped to his knees for a series of passes, each time working a little closer to the horns. He seemed self-destructive, as if he wanted the bull to kill him, virtually daring it to do so. Yet Catron wasn't watching. His eyes were closed, his thoughts elsewhere.

"The flesh is dead, but the spirit lives on."

He could see Paco Solorzano, lying on his back, his throat sliced and gaping so it resembled a grotesque second mouth beneath his chin, one that stood out amid a pool of drying blood, which was slowly turning from red to rust brown. The sword handler's words came back to him, as they'd been spoken in the Triana slums.

"Once I even had to go with him to Ireland . . . to attend some sort of stupid ritual. A Black Mass or something, the ceremony of some crazy cult."

Sublaran wasn't dead. He was alive, in some ectoplasmic state, just waiting to make his presence known. He was alive and taking his revenge on those who had forsaken him.

Had the old man found time to scream before the unexpected visitor brought the cold metal across his throat? Had he seen the blade coming toward him or felt it ripping through his flesh, carving a bloody line between life and death? Had he even known that at long last he was being made to pay a long-overdue debt he owed to his matador?

"Vengeance from beyond the grave. Other things besides heaven and earth, from out of the pits of hell."

Even more confusing than a rational motive was the identity of the killer and trying to discover such. Who had done the act? There were all sorts of possibilities. A vindictive relative of Cristo Cruz perhaps? After twenty years of silence? Why now? After so long?

"A maniac who needs no motive."

Catron's mind was at work, thinking up a story within the story, this time a fictional one, which was highly probable and happening in real life. A relative of the late Cristo Cruz, striking murderously upon all the associates of Jaime Sublaran still left alive. Irrational? Insane? Certainly, but to a deranged mind anything was possible.

"You think some nut is going to start killing Sublaran's associates?" Catron asked the group. "Revenge from a crazy man's point of view?"

No one answered. They were watching Sublaran, profiling, taking aim with the sword. One step, two, three. The steel went deep into the animal's back, between the shoulder blades, sinking until only the red taped hilt remained. The perfect kill, quick and decisive. Sublaran turned, watching as his horned adversary crumpled to the sand, spurting blood from its mouth and nose.

"The guy was good," Freddie acknowledged.

The next series of shots showed Sublaran taking a lap around the ring, smiling, celebrating his triumph, as he held the bull's severed ears in his hands. Although the silence of the room was penetrated only by the noise of the projector, Catron could hear the chanting of the thousands of fans, in a bullfight that had taken place almost a quarter century before.

"Sublaran! Sublaran! Sublaran! Sublaran! Sublaran! Sublaran!"

They were cheering for him then. It was before they turned on him. He was still their idol. He had all the world kissing his ass.

"What the hell was he doing at a Druid ritual?"

Catron could not shake loose the question evoked by Paco Solorzano. Druid? What would a Spaniard such as Sublaran have to do with a pagan cult attributed to an entirely different country and culture? Was he into the occult? A member of the Druid coven, still existing in modern times, centuries after they were thought to be extinct? A dabbler in the black arts? One who may have sold his soul to the devil for certain favors? A demonist or worse?

"Sublaran! Sublaran! Sublaran! Sublaran!"

The chant was very audible, but changing, growing distorted with each repetition until it resembled not a name, but a series of words in a foreign tongue, one he did not recognize. Where the picture of Jaime Sublaran had been, there was now something new, a group of men in black hoods, encircling a fire. For several minutes the ritual continued, his attention focusing on one of the members in the back of the coven. As his vision brought him closer to the hooded figure's face, he could see him, reaching up, removing the cloth mask to reveal his identity.

In the light of the fire, he could vaguely make out the features of Jaime Sublaran, looking much as he did in the oil painting. The face was the same, as was the hair, but there was something different in the eyes. They were glowing, beckoning to him. Then the matador spoke, one word, scarely above a whisper.

"Poder!"

Power! He was saying "power."

"He wasn't normal anymore. He was sick. I knew it long before the magazine photo came out."

Paco Solorzano had said it, but now he was dead. The how or why didn't matter, just the simple fact that he no longer walked the earth. The traitor was dead, the one who dared to hint of Sublaran's hidden secrets.

"Poder!"

"What did you say, Phil?" Freddie asked.

Catron found himself snapped back to reality. On the screen, the scene had changed again. It looked different, out of place. Another matador, not Sublaran, was leaning his head against the bullring's wooden fence, crying.

"Cristo Cruz!"

The words weren't necessary, although they shot into Catron's mind. He knew who the other matador was, long before he started the show. The reels were labeled. He'd singled this particular film out on purpose.

"Cristo Cruz became power mad. He had a little taste of glory, then he wanted to hog the whole cup."

Catron thought for a moment. What had made him say that? An inner opinion? A quote from somewhere recropping in his mind? Something from Solorzano? No, the old man had said a lot of things, but not that. It was a new voice, inside his head, yet not belonging there.

"Solorzano, get me some pictures of this."

Not knowing what to expect, Patsy screamed and the two men jolted in their seats as they watched crying Cristo Cruz shove a Civil Guard against the bullring wall, snatch his gun, and blow the top of his head off, the entire scene captured on film, just as it had happened in Huelva.

"Damn," Catron mused, transfixed by the turn of events in the movie. "He put more holes in his head than a woodpecker puts in a tree."

Patsy and her husband got up and left the study without a word. Freddie, too stunned to move, watching as the last bit of film ran out, leaving only the reflection of yellow light against the screen.

"Get up and flip on the lights," Catron ordered, as he rose from his seat. "I've got to rewind this."

Freddie, recovered slightly from the shock of just seeing a man commit suicide on the screen, was in no mood for more films, which he was afraid Catron might try to impress upon him and quickly obeyed the command, taking it as an excuse to make it to the door and exit. As the lights came on, Catron fidgeted hastily, rewinding the film, then rethreading it again.

"What the hell you doing?" Freddie asked, dumbfounded. He couldn't believe what he was seeing. Catron looked at him with a frustrated glance, then went back to resetting the projector.

"Jesus, Phil, you just saw a guy blow his brains out and you want to see it again?"

Catron paused, looking up from his work, confusion in his own face. He was beginning to sweat.

"Yeah, Freddie. Why not?"

Freddie screamed, his frustration overflowing. "Why not! You crazy bastard, that wasn't a damned Hollywood movie! That was for real! That guy shot himself!"

Catron slumped back into his seat, pouting. His friend didn't move or change his look of disgust. For several seconds, neither of them spoke. It was Freddie who broke the silence.

"You've got a heart of ice and ice water pumping through your veins, Phil. Your work's getting to you again."

"Hit the lights on the way out," Catron said.

Freddie turned and left the study, slamming the door behind him without another word. Catron watched with disinterest as he left. Opinions of other people never bothered him. Looking up at the picture, he smiled and spoke, addressing it. The routine was fast becoming a habit with him.

"You caused that to happen, didn't you? You got into his mind, just like you're getting into mine. I know you did it. You're the one who killed Solorzano too. No one human did it. You entered his mind, told him to pick up a knife, and cut his own throat, and he did it, didn't he?"

The picture remained mute and unchanged. After all, it was only a picture, a created image of oil paint and canvas. Catron considered this, then began to realize just how silly his statements had been. The more he thought about it, the more he understood what had been taking place. His project was overrunning him, yet in spite of his fixation, he had gotten little work done.

"I'll type all night," he resolved. "But first, I want to see this film again."

He cast a glance up at the painting, recalling his vision of the matador, dressed in a satanic robe, with orange flames leaping up in the foreground.

"You approve?" he questioned, waiting for the painting to respond. "Good, shall we begin?"

Catron rose and went to the light switch, but as he reached to turn it off, he felt a cold breeze behind his back, causing him to tense. Wind? It was impossible. Not in the house. He turned, halfway expecting to see a glowing spirit behind him, rattling a chain or perhaps more appropriately, carrying the ears of a bull.

"Empty?" he muttered, studying the painting one last time before shutting off the light. "No one here but me."

In the room's blackness, he had an extremely hard time finding his way back to the desk, but eventually he made it. He even breathed a sigh of deep relief as he flicked on the projector lamp, throwing the yellow reflection in a bright square across the screen. Never before had he been afraid of the dark, but this time he was glad, even for that one flicker of light. In the isolated study, he was the only person there, but somehow he felt that he wasn't completely alone. It was not a comfortable feeling, one attributed to children afraid of sleeping by themselves after watching a scary movie or during a thunderstorm, but totally unbecoming an adult.

"The flesh is dead, but the spirit lives on."

The phrase was becoming monotonous, getting on his nerves, but still he continued to use it. It kept coming back in his mind and trying his damnedest, he still couldn't figure where it was he'd first heard it.

"The spirit lives on," he repeated, shaking his head from side to side, feeling mild displeasure with himself. "The flesh is dead, but the spirit lives on."

With the touch of his index finger, he started the forward switch and the film clicked through the projector, bringing forth the image of bullfighters making their way across the bullring. Jaime Sublaran grinned as if he knew in advance what was going to happen that afternoon, resembling a child with a well-guarded secret. Next to him, on his right side, walked Cristo Cruz, smiling as he ignorantly headed toward his own death.

# 7

# OUT OF THE PAST

It was only when Phil Catron entered the house's attic that he realized his biggest mistake. While seeking outward resources, such as films, magazine articles, and associates in an effort to gather material on Jaime Sublaran, he had overlooked the inner sources, the biggest of which was right beneath the roof of the matador's mansion.

The attic was virtually a bullfighting museum, as he found by opening the boxes and built-in closets, pulling the contents out for his examination. There were over a dozen glittering costumes that Sublaran had worn into the ring, plus capes, swords, banderillas, and a picador's spear-tipped pole. Aside from the equipment were uncountable artifacts serving as a reminder that during his heyday, the matador was as marketable as any product, if not more so. There were Jaime Sublaran dolls, Jaime Sublaran coloring books, Jaime Sublaran calendars, and even rubber Jaime Sublaran masks, all stored away, waiting for someone to discover them.

Yet there was disappointment for Phil Catron. Though he had found many interesting things, there was nothing to confirm the rumors Paco Solorzano had planted in his mind, about the dark secrets of Jaime Sublaran.

"He wasn't normal anymore. He was sick."

Maybe they were just that? Rumors! Nothing more! Lies created by a stunned general public who did not know how to deal with the likes of the controversial matador.

"No contracts with the devil found so far," Catron mused as he held a Jaime Sublaran doll toward one of the lights. "No satanic bibles, no severed goats' heads, nothing. Just more trivia. Interesting, but still nothing beneath the surface. Where's all the proof to incriminate the big, bad, warlock matador anyway?"

He tossed the doll to the floor and sat back on one of the trunks, thinking. The longer he did so, the more he realized there was little to think about.

Junk? It gave him hints about the bullfighter's personality, that he was an egotist who kept anything to do with his name, including dolls, magazines, and coloring books, but that was something he already knew. The material was there and he should have looked for it sooner, but it still wasn't enough. It wasn't satisfactory. Somewhere there was a hidden key. He knew it. He could sense it, like the air before a storm, something to help him blow the mysterious tomb protecting the true secret life of Jaime Sublaran wide open, but where?

"He must have been quite a character. So rich, yet so dismal."

From what he'd figured, a cloud of foreboding hovered over Sublaran. It was obvious in the newspaper articles, from the contacts like Solorzano, and in the painting which hung in the study. Something more than tragic, a darkness, not a hideous, devil-horned evil, at least on outward appearance, but subtly sinister. Even the doll had it, that hard, depressed face, illuminated by only a forced grin. From what he'd heard, Sublaran wasn't a man for smiling. The only real smile he ever had was when Cristo Cruz shot himself in Huelva, and if at that moment he had something to smile about, it hadn't lasted long, for it had marked the downhill turning point of his own career. He could hear Solorzano and his words, back in the cantina.

"God help me, I filmed it all . . . and as I did, that madman was laughing!"

Catron shook his head, glancing down at the doll on the floor. If the real Sublaran looked anything like the miniature effigy, he couldn't picture him as the laughable type. From all accounts, he looked sombre, even sourful. He closed his eyes, thinking of the dream he'd had the night before, and everything that had happened since his arrival in Spain.

He was cracking, losing touch with reality, obsessed with his work and loosening his grip on the world. There was something about Sublaran, about his very house, that sent cold chills throughout his body. There was even something peculiar about the attic, but he couldn't pinpoint it regardless of how he tried. Like the secretive second life of the deceased matador, away from the arenas, it remained hidden, unnoticed by his conscious mind, just out of reach.

"Maniac."

The word came softly in Catron's mind, then again, with more emphasis.

"Maniac."

For the moment, he could not differentiate whether he meant to apply the word to the matador or to himself. He was looking down at the Sublaran doll, into the eyes. Behind their animated pupils was the same mournful bitterness as in the painting. Sad and painfilled on the outside, yet inwardly, burning with ambition for power and a willingness to destroy anyone who would interfere with his reaching these goals. He could see it plainly, no doubt whatsoever.

"Maniac."

The dream had been so vivid, he'd risen with a scream stuck in his throat. He was back with Sublaran, not in a bullring, but in a satanic circle. The people around him were partaking in a mock communion, a Catholic mass, only contrary in every ritual. The participants crossed themselves backwards, instead of consecrated wine, they took and drank from a vase containing water. Instead of a communion wafer, they had some hard, distasteful substance unknown to him. Yet the figures willingly partook of the service, sickening and perverse as they appeared to be, a secret Black Mass, just like in the novels about witchcraft.

"Our father who art in hell, hallowed by thy name, thy kingdom come, thy will be done, on Earth as it is in hell. Give us this day all that we ask and reward us our trespasses as we take revenge upon those who trespass against us. Lead us not into temptation and deliver us from good, for thine is the kingdom of the power and the glory, forever."

Dreams. If only there was some proof. A top matador, selling his soul to the devil, would make his book a best-seller. People were into scandal now more than ever, yet he could find no evidence, only speculation.

"Yet that day in Madrid, he went into the chapel to pray."

What had happened that particular afternoon, in Madrid's Plaza de Toros los Ventas? Why had it happened? Did Paco Solorzano know more about the secret practices of Jaime Sublaran than he'd told? If so, why had he remained so quiet for so long, and why had he died so suddenly? Who had killed him or had he killed himself? If so, again the question of why remained.

"What is it? Something's wrong with this house? With this attic."

Catron tapped the top of the trunk he was sitting on, and then it hit him. He lifted his hand toward the light, to see only his flesh, without a black mark of any kind.

Dust! There was no dust in the attic, no cobwebs, no dirt or mold. Though he knew the maid didn't clean there, the place was immaculate. That was the difference, the one that had troubled him but he couldn't figure out. It was an attic that was dust free, though apparently closed for years.

Again, he ran his finger against the trunk's surface, hoping to find a stain, a speck of dirt, anything, but it was clean. A phenomenon? Impossible? The logic said yes, but there had been a lot of funny things going on, too many things.

"The flesh is dead, but the spirit lives on."

Catron shook the statement from his mind. It was a joke, that's what it was. Freddie. No, Dennis and Patsy. They'd done it before leaving, to pry on his nerves. The bastards. He remembered them going, remembered their agreement.

"Bastards!"

Dennis and Patsy wanted to see Portugal, so they'd gone for the week, leaving Freddie and him behind. It was Freddie's idea to go to the Sunday bullfight. Nothing else was planned. While Patsy and her gorillalike husband were parading around having the time of their lives, wanting to be alone with each other, he was stuck busting his ass on research and entertaining the ape's halfwit manager. At least Freddie had paid for the bullfight tickets, front row, providing some compensation for his trouble.

"Phil, I know you get moody and irrational at times, but I should

beat the shit out of you for saying stuff about my wife like that,"
Catron mimicked his brother-in-law. "Blow it out your ass."

A clever joke. That's what they'd pulled off. Figuring he'd be
up in the attic sooner or later, they'd cleaned it out while he was
working. Probably they would have put a plastic skeleton in one
of the boxes too, had they the time. Scare the hell out of him? That's
what it was all about. Make him think the house was haunted, that
he was living in a retirement home for disgruntled spirits and
vampires.

"All we need now is a ghost running around rattling chains,"
he mused sarcastically, nudging the doll with his foot. He didn't like
the way it was looking at him, staring with its painted eyes, just
like the goddamned oil portrait. "This house is haunted enough
without outside help."

"He had no religion that I know of, but outwardly he bordered
on satanic."

He remembered the quote from Solorzano now, but couldn't find
any documented proof of it. In spite of all his efforts, he had found
very little meaning to anything evolving around Jaime Sublaran.
Rising, he started for the staircase, when another thought hit him.

"Right beneath you."

The trunk he'd been sitting on hadn't been opened. For some
reason, he hadn't bothered with it. Turning, he started toward it,
but as he reached the unlocked latch, another thought came to mind.
He remembered his own words.

"Probably they would have put a plastic skeleton in one of these
boxes too, had they the time."

What if they had put something in there, hoping he'd find it?
Or worse, what if there was something else within the trunk,
something dark and slithery, a hell spawn brought back to Spain
by Sublaran, from one of his weird ceremonies. He could open the
top and unleash a hoard of plagues upon mankind, just like in the
Greek myth, the one about Pandora's box.

"The flesh is dead," he whispered to himself as he reached for
the trunk, then pulled back again, fighting, trying to decide.

"Probably just more junk."

At that point he could sympathize with Pandora's plight, for his own curiosity was pushing him forward, egging him on. He had to open it, had to find out what was inside. He took the latches, flipping them open, then raised the lid . . .

"Pandora's box!"

The lid was open and nothing had jumped out. No flying pixies or elves. No demons reaching out with spaded claws to rip his flesh and muscles away. No flames, smoke, or burning brimstone from the pits of hell. There was only a book and a few sealed cigar boxes.

"Phil, are you up there?"

The voice came from the bottom of the stairs. Freddie Harmon. The troublemaker hadn't come out of the box like Greek mythology. He'd come down the hall, to the foot of the attic stairs.

"No!" Catron shot back impatiently. "I went to hell to try and sell an air conditioning system to the devil. Who do you think's up here? Jaime Sublaran?"

There was no answer from below, and this irritated him further. He let go with another wisecrack, more vehement than the previous one.

"Phil died. This is Jaime Sublaran . . . back from the grave. I'm coming to get you and take you to hell with me!"

Again, there was no reply. Then it came. "Just wanted to say I picked up the bullfight tickets I'd reserved, smartass. Tomorrow afternoon we're going, remember!"

Catron sighed and reached into his pocket, pulling out a pack of Celtas. He'd started smoking again, with no regrets whatsoever. Making his way toward the attic's exit, while he fidgeted putting a cigarette in his mouth and reinserting the pack back where it belonged, he felt his temper growing hot. There was no real provocation, but Harmon was annoying, just like the others, if not worse. People always irritated him when he was working. That's why he liked to be alone, isolated, when he wrote, free to do as he wanted without distraction. There were footsteps. Harmon was coming up the stairs.

"What the hell you want now?" Catron snarled, looking down where he could see the wrestling manager. "I'm working. Leave me alone."

"Screw yourself, then," Harmon answered with equal

vehemence, turning away. His footsteps echoed as he walked down the stairs and disappeared. Catron listened, waiting until he was sure the intruder was gone, then flicked the ashes off his cigarette and started toward the trunk. As he reached the lid, an odd thought hit him. It was closed.

"What the hell," he muttered. "No. If it was open before, then I must have shut it. I must have."

His eyes squinted as he tried to think back. Did he or didn't he shut the box when he heard Harmon coming up the stairs? He must have closed the lid. He absolutely must have.

"The spirit lives on somewhere in this house."

He felt something beneath his foot, throwing him off balance, as he heard a sharp crack. Looking down, he found the Jaime Sublaran doll, its plastic head shattered. He'd accidentally stepped on it. Destroyed it? No, killed it! The doll was dead, just like its namesake, with its face crushed in.

"The flesh is dead."

No question about that. He's seen the picture, wondering what the face, blotched out in all the published photographs, had really looked like after the goring. The horn had done tremendous damage before killing him, mashing his skull, just like the sole of his shoe had smashed the plastic doll.

As he stared down at the broken thing, Catron felt a shot of pity course through his body. It was only a doll, but somehow he felt like he had destroyed something more sacred. There was no other word to describe it. Combining this with the illogically immaculate attic and the feelings that had troubled him since he started the Sublaran project, he began to wonder if it was all his imagination or if somehow the ghost stories he's heard about haunted houses since he was a little kid were true after all.

"Just like in the monster movies," he repeated, flicking the remains of his cigarette away and grinding the butt out with his foot. Beside the mashed Celta, the doll looked literally pathetic, like a miniature war victim, splattered over the trenches and blood-stained ground of a battlefield.

"To hell with it all," he sighed, opening the trunk once again. "Spooks, come and get me!"

# 8

# THE BULLFIGHT

Phil Catron and Freddie Harmon sat in the front row of Huelva's bullring in the shady section, the most expensive seats in the house. The entire stadium was vibrating with the nervous anticipation that came before every bullfight. The people in the stands were waiting, from the costly seats to the cheapest at the top tier, for the trumpet call had come, signaling the start of the spectacle, just like at a race track. When it blasted out, high and blaring from a solitary trumpeter, and the red gates on the opposite side of the ring opened, the applause was deafening. As the music swelled about them, the three matadors stepped into the ring and started their march across the sand.

Juanito Montana was the most experienced of the matadors, walking on the left side of the procession, dressed in a suit of black and gold. Next to him, in the middle, was Ramos Delgado from Portugal, wearing lime green and silver. On the right end was the third matador, Mario Romero. He came from San Sebastian, in northern Spain, and was wearing a costume of purple and gold. Neither Delgado nor Romero had much of a following. It was Montana who had the most prowess. He was the star of the show, the one the people came to see.

"Montana will fight the first and fourth bull," Harmon explained with authority. "Delgado will fight the second and the fifth, Romero the third and sixth."

Catron looked at him with a smirk and shook his head. "Man,

I've seen these things before. I know what the hell's going on. I'm working on a book, remember?''

Harmon turned away in annoyance, diverting his thoughts and attention back to the sand. He was trying to be friendly, but it wasn't paying off. When he looked back, he saw Catron lighting a cigar.

"What you smoking that turd for," he asked sarcastically. "Those things stink."

"Wrestlers stink too," Catron answered between clenched teeth as he struck a match, "but you still hang around them, don't you?"

Another trumpet call sounded and a smaller door was opened, just below their seats. Momentarily, there was nothing, then a cry of awe arose from the crowd as six hundred kilos of snorting black bull rocketed from the tunnel into the ring, the grain yellow and green ribbons of Don Eduardo Miura's ranch blowing in colorful streams off its back.

"Horned death," Catron muttered, thinking of the bull that had killed Jaime Sublaran. "All the power and the glory."

Montana let the bull circle the ring twice, studying every movement the noble beast made. Each bull was different, with its own style of charging. Most favored one horn more than the other. Some had poor eyesight. Others would paw the sand and bellow, bluffing before deciding to attack. The matador had only a short amount of time to determine these things to the best of his ability, but he had to take them into consideration. Failure to notice a slight hooking habit with the right or left horn, a sign of faulty vision, or the tendency of the bull to veer away from the cape and toward the man's legs had caused more than one fatal goring.

"The bull is good," Harmon acknowledged. "This is why I came to Spain. This is what I wanted to see. It will be a . . . "

Montana stepped out from behind the fence, flaunting the bull's charge. Each time the bull passed him, he swung the cape away and the crowd screamed with satisfaction. They called it the veronica pass, named after Saint Veronica, who allegedly wiped the face of Christ with a cloth on his way to the cross. Evidently, whoever dubbed this piece of capework in her honor must have assumed that when she wiped Jesus's bloody face, she had been holding the cloth matador style. It seemed almost a sacrilege.

After the last pass, Montana walked away and another trumpet call sounded, signaling the time of the picadors. The gates were opened and two of them came riding in, their sharpened poles poised. Upon seeing them, the bull was by no means hesitant with his attack. It dove toward the nearest mounted man, sinking its horns into the quilted padding draped over the horse's side for protection, trying futilely to gore this new target. As it slammed into the horse, the picador leaned forward, driving the speartip into its back muscles. Some of the tourists grew squeamish at this time, but Catron watched in morbid fascination. From the wide puncture, the blood began to flow. First blood of the fight.

He shut his eyes, thinking. A blood sacrifice. The bullfight itself was little more than a pagan ritual. Someone would die in the end, always. There could be no other way. Be it from man or bull, blood was always a necessity.

Cristo Cruz, for instance, had been the ultimate sacrifice, here in this very bullring. Thoughts of him blowing his brains all over the passageway, captured on film, reentered his mind. The blood had shot out from the bullet holes, not pumping as in the case of the bull's penetrated hide, but spurting, literally flying. It had made a pattern, an angelic blood halo, mocking the crown of thorns placed on the head of Christ.

Oblivious to the pain, the bull kept prodding at the horse, until Montana intervened, flicking his cape to divert the animal's attention, leading it away across the ring to the spot where the other picador was waiting and the process was repeated.

Catron choked on a puff of cigar smoke. He was sweating, not feeling well. In the back of his head there was a pounding. A headache was coming on. Rather than being at the bullfight, he now would have preferred to be at the house. The spell had been coming on all day, gradually working toward a climax. First the dull thud, now open pain.

A fourth trumpet call shot across the top of the bullring and the picadors were ushered from the arena. It was time for the banderillas.

"Montana puts them in sometimes," Harmon said. Catron shrugged, and took the cigar from his mouth, blowing out a thin film of smoke.

The crowd grumbled when they saw an elderly man dressed in a shabby costume of pink and black, which was too tight for him, threatening to split at the seam. It was one of Montana's banderilleros. Something about him didn't make the crowd happy, for the grumbling grew louder, then a single voice, from somewhere, above the others.

"Montana!"

Another voice picked up the name, then another. Soon it was a chant, booming from every seat like cannon fire.

"Montana! Montana! Montana! Montana! Montana!"

The old banderillero looked quizzically at the matador, who was watching from behind the wooden fence. Inspired by the clamor, a smile crossed his face, but he was waiting, wanting the noise to grow louder still.

"They want him to put in his own banderillas," Harmon explained, picking up the chant himself.

"Montana! Montana! Montana! Montana! Montana! Montana!"

The matador stepped from behind the barrier and motioned for his banderillero. The old man ran toward him, handing him the paper-covered sticks, while the crowds responded with joyous roar. Montana held the banderillas high, for everyone to see, then motioned toward the arena band. Music! He wanted music. There was a short delay before the musicians caught the drift of things, then came the lonely wail of the opening notes "La Ultima Estocada."

Catron stiffened in his seat as he recognized the song, thinking back to the study where he had heard it on Sublaran's record player. "La Ultima Estocada"—twenty years before, it had been Jaime Sublaran's theme. Now, having forgotten him, they were making it Montana's. A surge of anger went through him, like Sublaran himself must have felt when Cristo Cruz threatened to steal a glimmer of the limelight.

"Solorzano, get me some pictures of this," Catron mouthed.

"What?" Harmon said, turning his head. "What did you say? I don't have a camera."

"I want to remember what happened to this fraud who thought he could rival me."

"Phil, what the hell are you talking about? You're making me miss the action."

Montana ran toward the bull, the banderillas poised. Just as the animal looked certain to catch him, he feigned with his leg, diverting the charge and the horn went past him. Just as the tip sliced by his embroidered jacket, he brought his arms down, placing the two sticks perfectly in the bull's back. Dancing away, with a grin on his face, the matador accepted the praise of the crowd, the cheers and applause mingled with the music of "La Ultima Estocada," in all of its passion.

"Keep filming, damn you," Catron said, louder, causing the people around him to stare. His eyes were getting glassy. "I'll tell you when I want you to stop."

Harmon looked at him and flinched, not understanding the command. Below him, the matador was taking the second pair of banderillas, holding them up as before, for the crowd to see. Then, unexpectedly, he brought them down against the fence, snapping the shafts in half. Cortos! He was placing cortos banderillas, the broken ones, making the danger more obvious. Catron was watching him with an idiotic look, as if in a drunken stupor. Freddie turned away from him. He had paid to see the bullfight and that's what he was going to see.

Slowly, Montana made his way toward the bull, one step at a time, in a reproduction of Sublaran's famous Cat Walk. Then as the bull started to charge, he turned his own gingerlike steps into a full run.

"Solorzano," Catron screamed, rising to his feet. "Get me a picture of this."

Before Freddie or anyone else could pull him down, the whole audience was rising, screaming. The horn caught Montana high inside the right leg, lifting him upward. He spun on the horn, then the animal shook its head, throwing him off. Capes were flashing everywhere, trying to distract the bull from the prostrate matador. It made one more attack, trampling him beneath its hooves, before being led away to the section of seats directly below Catron. In the confusion, no one noticed him stripping off his suit coat, or the wide smile on his face. Their attention was glued to the matador, who was on his knees, holding his groin.

As two banderilleros reached the injured bullfighter, scooping him up with their hands under his armpits, one could easily see where the wound had been made. His entire right pants leg was torn, but beneath the ripped silk was another jagged hole, this one some seven inches deep, located in flesh, not fabric, and starting to bleed.

"It's got him," Harmon said, almost mournfully. "He's been gored."

Two others came into the arena, lifting the matador's feet. All eyes watched as the gored Montana was carried from the ring and rushed to the infirmary where the bullring doctors were already preparing for surgery. While this was going on, Catron had shifted the coat in his hands, so he now held it matador style, capelike, in front of him.

His eyes were shut. He was thinking, not of Montana's goring, but another, far worse, that had taken place in Madrid, long before. Jaime Sublaran was flat on his back, as Montana had been. The horns were bearing down on the injured man, who saw them coming. Feebly, he put his arms in front of his face, as if to shield himself, but the defense wasn't strong enough. The horn entered in the side of his face, tossing him across the sand, sending him skidding in a mass of silk, gold spangles, and flying dust. He looked like a life-size rag doll, getting his stuffings torn out, for the animal caught him again, under the jaw, lifting him slightly and dragging him on the ground, while the hardest of men hid their eyes and others vomited.

The ring workers rushed to carry the man away. He had virtually no face left. His upper body and what was left of his head were bathed in blood, as if someone had dumped a bucket of red paint over the top of him. His mouth was open, wide and breathless, but it was hard to tell exactly where his mouth was, due to the long gash which had ripped from the nape of his neck to the temple. His left eye stared up, sightlessly at the sky, standing out like a white pearl amid the glistening blood. Next to it, where the right eye should have been, there was only a grisly hole, leading back into the punctured brain.

He thought of the picture hanging in the study and how different the matador looked. Before and after, a grim parody on the television, weight-reducing commercials back in the United States,

# 9

# BERSERK

The first thing Catron grew aware of was the painful throbbing in the back of his head, an acute series of sledgehammer blows which forced him to open his eyes. There above him was the sky, blue and cloudless, and below it, row upon row of concrete seats. He was in a bullring, but not Huelva's. This one was larger. Barcelona? Sevilla? Madrid!

He turned around, rolling off the position on his back in which he had found himself, rising to his knees and looking upward to study his surroundings better. It was then he noticed another change.

His eyes caught a glittering on his sleeve, not from his blue business suit, but the embroidered, black and gold material from a bullfighter's costume. As he examined himself more carefully, he found to his surprise he was wearing an expensive matador's suit of lights.

"Well, I'll be damned and sent to hell," he muttered, pulling himself to his feet. "Everything's different."

He began to tour the empty ring, trying to place this new location by examining the interior. There must have been well over twenty thousand seats, tier after tier of them, and there was only one bullring in Spain that size. It was indeed the Plaza de Toros los Ventas in Madrid. Alone on the huge circle of sand, he felt insignificant, like an ant at the bottom of an empty vase, or an insect being studied through a microscope.

Everything was quiet, too quiet, the only noise being an occasional ripple of wind. There were no cheers, no notes of music, no snorts and bellows from an angry bull. The place was empty and as silent as a cemetery once all the mourners had gone home.

"Now how in the name of hell did I get here?" Catron marveled, placing his hands on his hips. The black and gold costume fit snugly. It was somewhat difficult to move in. "What in the name of hell, heaven, and earth is going on."

He looked off into the sunlight, trying to distinguish if there was anyone else in the bullring who could answer his question. His head was hurting terribly, making him dizzy. For a moment he thought he was going to lose his balance and fall, but he caught himself against the bullring's wooden fence, steadying his stance. From his unstable position, he could feel the earth move beneath him, falling away. He grasped the fence harder, looking up into the stands, hoping he could see something familiar. Then the alarming question hit him with all its force. If he didn't know how he'd gotten there, how was he going to get back?

Then he saw someone, another figure, watching silently from the opposite side of the arena. Catron turned to face him, slumping backward against the fence, to prop himself up as he spoke.

"Who are you?"

The figure didn't answer, but he started walking toward him, closer, looking down, his face obscured. He was also wearing a matador's costume and his hands were held behind his back, as if to hide something.

"Who are you?" Catron repeated, but the figure kept coming. Again he said it, louder, then finally as a scream. "Who the hell are you? What am I doing here?"

The figure, now only a few yards away, looked up, revealing the face of Cristo Cruz.

"Oh, my God," Catron cried, but he was sure that where he was, God could not hear him. "Oh, my God. Oh, my God. Oh, my God."

Smiling, the matador brought forth his hands, revealing what he'd hidden behind his back, a civil guard's miniature submachine gun. Without a word, he fitted the gun beneath his chin and pulled the trigger.

Catron wanted to close his eyes, to scream, to move, to run, but something held him in his place. He could only watch as Cristo Cruz was lifted off his feet, falling backward to the sand, blood shooting from his wounds as the bullets pumped through his head, showering the air in an explosion of gore, brain matter, and skull fragments.

Catron gagged, spinning around to hang doubled up over the fence, feeling the urge to vomit overcoming him. As he turned back, he saw the figure sprawled out on the ground, outlined by a silhouette of blood . . . and moving.

The thing was rising. It was getting up. It hadn't been killed, but how could it be? It had been dead over twenty-five years ago. It couldn't be killed or kill itself, because it was already dead.

The creature's face was still distinguishable, but the top of its head was at a peculiar angle, lopsided, like a carelessly placed toupee. He could see the holes, actually see where the bullets had gone, and the distortion of the thing's jaw. It just stood there, facing him, doing nothing, then to his horror, he saw it point the gun, straight in his direction, and he was looking down the bore.

"Noooo!" he screamed, falling in a huddle against the fence. He was prepared for the worst, to feel the bullets ripping into him, the lead penetrating his flesh, tearing his life away. But there was nothing. It seemed forever before he found the courage to open his eyes, and when he did, the creature was gone. The bullring was empty, like before.

He rose, quickly, the seam of the matador's pants starting to give away. It didn't matter. He had only one thought in mind, to get away, out of this hellhole, this nightmare which was coming true.

"Help me," he found himself shouting. "Get me out of here! I'm not ready to die."

From high above, he heard the call of a trumpet, blurting out the opening notes of "La Ultima Estocada," but it was impossible. There was no band.

"Get me out of here," he babbled. "Get me out. Get me out. Get me out."

His pleas turned into a high-pitched shriek of horror. At the opposite side of the bullring the gate was open. It was the tunnel from where the bulls were let into the ring. He could hear the words now, plainly, in his mind, in English, yet in a different voice, foreign to him.

"Death waits behind that door . . . with sharp horns and fast hooves. You're going to meet death now, horned death. Hell lies behind that door and from that door a demon is coming. You're going to meet the hell spawn now. He's from the ranch of Miura. He's waiting for you. You're his enemy and he's going to kill you."

From out of the dark hole shot a bull, bigger and blacker than he'd ever seen. On its flank, it wore the brand of Miura, in its back the ribboned colors, which flopped a mock flamenco dance as the animal came. Its horns were as wide as the handlebars on a bicycle and as it made its way into the arena, corral dust blew off its hide, giving it a mystic, godlike appearance. A bovine killing machine, alive, angry, parading around the ring in search of something to destroy.

Catron started to run, but he had only gotten a few paces when he fell to his face, his feet pulled out from under him. He tried to move, but couldn't get away. Something was holding him, actually holding him. In panic, he twisted, looking over his shoulder, and he nearly fainted in disbelief.

Two hands had come up from the ground, grasping his ankles to prevent him from escaping. He was trying to get away, but they held him pinned, while the bull drew closer to him. In that split second he saw everything, like people about to die reportedly see their lives flash before their eyes.

"Sublaran! Sublaran! Sublaran! Sublaran! Sublaran!"

The chanting filled the air, louder than the sounds of "La Ultima Estocada." The death grip around his ankles had tightened, as if two vices were holding him. The hands were barely human to his sensations, cold and clammy like those of a corpse. The plaza was filled with thousands of faceless people, chanting the name of Jaime Sublaran, watching expectedly as he was about to die.

At that point Catron wondered about his own identity. Who was Jaime Sublaran? Why had he such a fascination with the ill-fated matador? Had it been coincidence? No. He was chosen, in fact cursed, singled out to relive the fate of the excommunicated bull-fighter. He was in hell and he was Jaime Sublaran. Phil Catron didn't exist. He never had. It was Sublaran all along.

The words made no sense. Nothing did. The bull was almost upon him, drawing nearer, its horns lowered. He raised his arms, throwing them over his head as Sublaran had done in a futile attempt to protect himself. Yet he knew it would do no good. The bull would plow through this flimsy barrier. The horn would catch him, driving straight through his eye and into the brain. Then, though he was already dead, he would be thrown around like a child's toy. The horn would catch him under the jaw and rip off half the side of his face, before anyone could rescue him.

"The bull kept hooking into his face, again and again, destroying him."

"Sublaran couldn't have been buried in the traditional way, even if he wanted to. He was excommunicated."

Jaime Sublaran was dead, just like Cristo Cruz. Just like Paco Solorzano. Just like Phil Catron was going to be.

"Play me 'La Ultima Estocada.' Play me the song of death!"

Then it happened. He only felt it for a second, the hot horntip burying into his eyeball, then the red, followed by instant blackness as his body was dragged roughly across the sand, already dead, yet kicking and spasming in violent muscular reaction.

"No! I can't be dead!"

Catron opened his eyes, to discover his surroundings had changed again. He was in another room, much smaller, and with bars, behind a cage. He was lying on a cot in a jail cell.

"God," he sighed, propping himself on his elbows. "It was just a dream."

At that point he noticed a guard staring at him from the other side of the bars. Next to him was Freddie Harmon.

"Okay, Manolete, let's go," he said coldly. "It took all night, but I got you out of this mess."

"I'm no Manolete," Catron muttered.

"You did a pretty good job of proving that yesterday. Who the hell'd you think you were, Jaime Sublaran?"

"What time is it?"

"Noon. Monday. Where the hell have you been, on a different planet than the rest of us?"

The guard unlocked the door and following the checkout process, the two men were walking down the streets of Huelva in search of a taxi to take them home. Neither of them spoke, until Harmon decided to break the silence.

"Man, what got into you yesterday?"

Catron thought for a moment, then shook his head. The picture of horns coming toward his face was still vivid in his mind, as was a solitary question. Had it really been a dream? By indication, the last adventure was, but the episode at the Huelva bullring certainly hadn't been.

"I don't know. One minute I was watching that Montana get carried out. The next minute I was in there with the goddamned bull."

"What got into you though? Were you drinking vodka all day?"

"I don't know. I just don't know. Call it an impulse."

"An impulse!" Harmon erupted. "You wind up in jail. You damn near get yourself killed. You cause a riot like you wouldn't believe, and you say it's all on account of a goddamned impulse! Are you out of your mind? You realize the shit storm I had to go through to get you out of this? They have laws against stunts like jumping into the bullring. This is Spain, not the United States of America. They don't give a damn who you are or who you think you are."

"Shut up or swing," Catron snarled suddenly, backing off. Freddie tensed.

"What did you say, Catron?"

"I said shut up or swing. I never took any shit from you before, and I don't plan on taking it now."

Harmon's eyes widened. He was angry, but cautious, not sure of what to think or do. His words were slow in coming, anticipating trouble. "What's wrong with you? If it wasn't for me, you'd still be in jail."

"If it wasn't for you and that trained gorilla who married my sister, I wouldn't be here at all," Catron answered, turning to walk away. A cab had come around the corner, but at the moment he didn't feel like sharing the ride with Freddie Harmon.

"You've got a brain the size of a splinter," he heard the shouting from behind. "Phil, you're a goddamned fruitcake, just like Dennis says. You're a fruitcake! A fruitcake! You have raisins for eyes!"

Catron ducked into a bar and bought a package of Celtas, watching from the window as Harmon got into the cab and headed down the street. The cigarette tasted good to him, better than ever. As he watched the film of smoke rising in front of his face, he was finally able to relax. He was still wearing the blue business suit from the previous day, now dirty and torn at one knee. His usually clean-shaven face was growing dark with traces of beard, his hair was ruffled, and it hurt whenever he moved his arms. In short, he looked like hell, yet no one paid him any mind.

"Cerveza?" the bartender asked. He was a short, fat little man, bald and happy looking.

"Sí," Catron nodded, the words escaping from the corner of his mouth, the side which didn't hold the cigarette. "Cerveza."

The man brought back a glass filled with beer from a tap and a side order of potatoes. It was the custom in small bars to give a complementary appetizer with each drink. Catron dropped some coins on the bar, more than was necessary, but he shrugged and waved the man away, when he attempted to give him change.

"Screw it," he said in English, but the bartender didn't understand. "Screw the change . . . no cambio . . . es por tu."

At that moment he began thinking back. He could hear his sister's voice, plain and vivid, just as it had sounded when she spoke.

"Phil, why don't you come with us? Dennis is paying for everything. He's taking me and his manager too. We're flying to Madrid then down to Huelva by train, where we're going to rent this big mansion for the whole summer. You need the rest, Phil. Why don't you go? It isn't costing you anything. Dennis wants you to come. We all do."

"Patsy," he answered. "I'll tell you why I don't come. Because all the time I'm there I'll have to listen to that caveman husband of yours and his halfwit manager crowing about how successful they've been, flopping around in a ring like a couple of beached whales. I don't need them telling me about how much money they made at Madison Square Garden or at the Philadelphia Spectrum or at the Devil's Union Hall, Local 13, in hell, with their damned wrestling program. And if I do go, I'll have the son of a bitch reminding me all the time that he paid for the trip. He lives to do things like that. He waits for chances where he can irritate me. He reaches out like he's going to help me across a pile of horseshit, then shoves me in. The guy's a jerk, and I'm not going.''

"You've always hated him, haven't you?''

"If you want me to tell the truth, yes, I have.''

"Why?''

"The bastard's always knocking me. Knocking what I do. He thinks I don't work. His ass. Just because he can't read, he has to cut down my writing. That's typical of him and everyone he associates with. If you want to lower yourself and be with his crew, fine, but don't drag me into the cesspool with you. I don't like the smell.''

"You're impossible,'' she screamed at him. "And Dennis knows how to read!''

Somehow, he'd still wound up going with them, on the pretense that it would be relaxing. Now there was a real horse laugh! Relaxing? He'd come close to dying, for no logical reason, and a nagging inside his mind told him the worst was yet to come.

"The house awaits me,'' he told himself, as he stared at his beer. There were bubbles in it, tiny things which fascinated him. "The house awaits, and three more days with Dennis Flagstaff's animal trainer, before heaven's couple returns from Portugal. Joy! Oh, great joy to end all joys.''

He hesitated, thinking of Harmon, the dumpy, stereotyped wrestling manager from the first green light. He'd grown up watching people like him and Flagstaff on obscure UHF stations, which always came in fuzzy but still picked up the image of ranting maniacs, swearing revenge upon their rivals and masked men pounding each other's heads into padded turnbuckles. It was the world of such luminaries as Gorgeous George, Flying Bill Anderson, The Exotics, Maniac Mike Gordon, and a thousand others like them. What a life!

"Screw you people,'' he sighed, imagining several unpleasant things he'd like to have seen happen to all of them. "Screw every last one of you and your meddling, interfering souls. You're dealing with things you don't understand, things bigger than any of you.''

He lifted his glass, but before he could taste the beer, he caught sight of something. Over the bar, directly in front of him, was a framed, black-and-white photo, distorted by a signature, so poorly scrawled he couldn't make out the name, but it wasn't necessary. The picture was of a matador, dressed in a shining costume and holding a bull's ear. The face was Jaime Sublaran's.

Without a word, Catron guzzled the beer and left the bar, heading back out into the street. The bartender watched him go, shaking his head in mild confusion as he took the empty glass and dropped it into the water-filled sink. He hadn't even bothered to eat the potatoes.

# 10

# FACE TO FACE

Once Catron arrived at the house, he changed clothes and went right to typing in the study, without bothering to eat or sleep. Harmon was nowhere to be found. From all available clues, he hadn't been there since morning. The maid, Carlotta, had made her weekly visit to the mansion and cleaned things, but had stayed away from the desk, where the typewriter and partially finished manuscript rested. It had been his expressed orders that nothing be disturbed.

With the music of one of the records playing in the background, Catron worked fast, listening to the songs and trying to name them as he typed. "El Gato Montez," "Pura Solera," "El Beso," "Manton De Manila," and naturally, "La Ultima Estocada," but the melodies didn't distract him. If anything, they helped him. Each time the record ended, he would reset it, then continue with his work, until late afternoon became early evening. He was going strong, better than ever, as he created the life story of Jaime Sublaran on paper.

He had wanted to visit the attic, but there would be time for that later on. At the moment, there was still much work to be done, now that he had the mood, the fire burning within him, enabling him to turn out paragraph after paragraph. Whatever blocks in the way of his writing had existed before, had suddenly been torn down, not a brick at a time, but with a bulldozer. As he continued, new thoughts were cropping up in his mind, curious ones that had never entered before. Other words from Paco Solorzano, which he had put aside, were suddenly vivid, troubling him as he worked on.

Evidently, Sublaran had been going to bed with a lot of people, providing the gossip was true, including the nuns. It didn't look good. Not at all. He could picture this unidentified nun from Mexico, lying dead with a gun in one hand, a picture of the matador in the other, and a bullet hole in the side of her head. What a scandal that must have made, one that for some reason or another had been successfully covered up, forgotten like a bad political maneuver.

He found himself wondering about Sublaran's women. What kind were they? European? American? African? Perhaps a mingling of all kinds. Who was the nun? Did she really exist? Was it a figment of Paco Solorzano's imagination or a fabricated piece of slander directed toward the late matador? Who was to say? With Solorzano dead, there was no source of information to help him pursue the fact, at least that he could come up with at the moment. Indeed, Jaime Sublaran was an enigma, one that could not be figured out completely. Each bit of fact heightened, rather than narrowed down, the great mystery surrounding him.

Yet the original furnishings of the house did not give away evidence that Sublaran was a womanizer, in spite of the gossip and the general romantic image that was attributed to most bullfighters. There were no pictures of women anywhere to be found in the house, just as there were no pictures of saints or religious articles. Those left alive who might have known something about all this were certainly reluctant to talk. In all instances, the man was blacklisted, avoided like a case of venereal disease. People didn't like the subject and cringed, especially when in Huelva, the name was mentioned. They preferred to talk instead of the positive elements, those who had influenced their town for good, like the Litri family and Columbus. How quickly they forgot that for over a decade Sublaran had been their idol, putting their unimportant city on the map. All the good was forgotten in favor of the bad.

Catron looked at the picture, which as usual stared down on him while he worked. There was no glow in the eyes anymore, just pigments of oil paint. That was all it ever was. A painting. Realizing this, he was free to do his work without being obsessed by the haunting memory of the matador, even capable of making jokes about him. He seemed to recall a warning about it being poor taste to make fun of the dead, but he'd never seen one corpse rise from the grave to complain. Who? Jesus maybe? That was it.

Still, there was a morbid fascination he held for the artwork, a mysteriousness about it that made the whole thing attractive. Yet he didn't know the name of the artist who had created the painting. The signature was illegible in the right hand corner, near the edge of the meeting point between canvas and frame. It was only an impression, but one which captured the matador's countenance and attitude to the letter. The face was gloomy, with only the trace of a smile, but nonetheless managed to vibrate with the majestic arrogance which had been Sublaran's trademark. The emperor of the bullring, monarch of a circular kingdom, ruler of the Plaza de Toros, where death in the afternoon sun was always a certainty in one form or another. Jaime Sublaran, looking down on him from the mantel, as he did his typing.

"What would you be thinking right now, matador?" Catron questioned. "We're face to face and still don't communicate. I'm trying to restore the honor to your name. You know that, don't you? Of course you do. You're putting ideas into my head, aren't you?"

He looked at the face, analyzing it and like the trick pictures he used to see in certain comic books, the ones that created optical illusions, this picture too was changing. The longer he stared, the more advanced the alterations became. Where the face had been that of Jaime Sublaran in all his glory, it now represented him in death. Blood covered his entire head, spilling down to his jacket and shirt as well. Where the right eye had been, there was now a bloody hole, empty and red. Next to the socket, the eyeball hung like a solitary grape, draping from thin tendons, about to fall off.

"Jesus," Catron hissed. "Jesus in heaven, it's happening again."

Sublaran's head was now twisted at the neck, drooping stupidly to the side. Beneath the distorted jawbone was a long entry wound where the horn had caught him one of the many times, hurling him across the arena floor.

Rather than shock or horror, Catron stared in utter amazement at the phenomenon, a ghost story come to life. Was it really happening? Or was he dreaming again? Hoping for the best, he closed his eyes, with a prayer that when he opened them things would be back to normal. As he looked a second time, he saw the picture had changed, only worse.

There was no longer the body of a matador butchered by the horns of the bull in front of him, but the painting of a rotting corpse dressed in the black and gold suit of lights, already in an advanced state of decomposition. Beneath the brow's flesh, pieces of shattered skull bone peeked through. The hair was frizzled and falling, like a fright wig, and the one remaining eye stared outward, beneath a moribund film. The mouth had dropped open, blending with the strips of peeled flesh and gashes which were crusted with age. The hands were like those of a leper, gnarled and covered with white sores. That sand in the horizon behind his back had turned to mud, a dark and boggy sea. Then he saw the worst of all.

Worms were coming out of the body. Through the skeletal nose and mouth, through the openings in the head that the horn had made, through the faded material of the costume and the silk parade cape. The air was filled with a ghastly, spoiled smell, a repulsive odor that made him choke. He closed his eyes, burying his head in his arms, crying.

"God, take this thing away!"

When at last he found the courage to look up, everything about the painting was normal, as he knew it would be. Shaking his head, he withdrew the piece of paper from the typewriter and rose to shut off the record player. It was time to quit for the evening.

Reading as he walked, he found something else which disturbed him, something written on the manuscript that he didn't remember typing. Two words, in English.

"I live."

He read them aloud, then crumbled the paper and tossed it to the floor. "The hell you say," he cursed, looking back at the picture. It was laughing at him, through that damnable expression, so mournful, yet so smug and confident at the same time. "The living hell, you say!"

Though he had destroyed the source, the message lingered on. He knew nothing could change that. It would be there for some time! Accepting this, he started out the drawing room for something to eat and then to go to bed, but the doorway was open, his path was blocked.

"I've got somewhere I want you to go tomorrow," Freddie Harmon said. Catron looked up at him quizzically.

"Where the hell you been?"

"At the hotel where Ramos Delgado was staying. Remember him, the other matador on the card, the Portuguese, who tried to save you when you jumped into the ring. Remember? He told me of a woman in Huelva you should go see."

"About the book?" Catron asked. "You told him about the book?"

Harmon hesitated, trying to choose his words carefully. He didn't do a good job.

"Yes, in a way. I told him about the book and how you've been acting, like you're possessed or something. I had to give him some kind of explanation, why you jumped into the ring."

"Why?" Catron questioned, anger starting to rise detectably in his voice. "Where's this son of a bitch now?"

"On his way back to Portugal."

"And he told you I should see who?"

"La Bruja."

"What the hell's La Bruja?"

Again Harmon hesitated, predicting the response. "She's a *gitana*. A gypsy fortune-teller."

"To hell with you," Catron responded, going back toward the desk. He was no longer tired or hungry. Anything, even working, was better than this conversation. He had no sooner inserted a page, than Harmon was leaning over the typewriter, stopping him. It was getting to be an annoying recurrence. First Dennis Flagstaff, now his manager. Catron looked up at him in exasperation and raised his eyebrows.

"I can't work with you holding the damned carriage down."

Harmon looked him square in the eyes. There was no anger, only bewilderment, perhaps even a hint of concern.

"I think you should let this story go, Phil."

Catron's face was chipped of stone. He didn't like this at all. "Why? Why should I let this story go? One good reason."

"Because you're diving nose first into a vat of bullshit, man. This obsession of yours is messing with your mind. You ain't right.

You're starting to act crazy. Nuts! You're acting like you ain't been dealt a full hand in the card game. It's all been happening since you started this story."

"I'll tell you where you're wrong," Catron shot back, reaching for another Celta. "I'm winning this card game, because the deck is stacked and I hold four aces. This is my story, and I'm busting my ass on it, because it's going to sell. It's going to make me famous, then I'll have all the money and the power. Do you understand?"

"Yeah, Phil, I understand," Harmon responded sadly. His warnings weren't sinking in. "You're the one who doesn't understand."

"Understand what? You're an expert on writing?"

"No, I'm an expert on life. There are some things that are better left alone, some stories that shouldn't be told. Sublaran's one of them. You don't know what a storm he raised. He's dead and buried now. It's over and best forgotten. Don't go digging up any corpses that are better off under the ground. Don't get involved in this scandal. Leave the bullshit to the flies."

Catron lit the Celta and sucked in, feeling the smoke swirl in his mouth. He was trying to look disinterested, but Harmon was pressing, still carrying on.

"Tomorrow we're going to see this old woman. She knew Sublaran. She predicted his death in the ring. She knew he was going to die. I got the story from Ramos Delgado. The woman's famous. She's been doing this a long time. Talk to her. Maybe she can tell you something about Jaime Sublaran."

Catron suddenly smiled. He'd caught the trap before it was set, jumping on the screw up, right when it came.

"That's strike one on you. You just missed the ball! One minute you tell me not to write this story about Jaime Sublaran. The next minute you try to talk me into going with you by telling me she can help me with my book. Harmon, don't bullshit a manure salesman. I don't know what you're trying to hide or trying to do, but it won't work. I'm not going anywhere outside this house. I've got plans of my own."

Harmon released his grip on the typewriter, but his position didn't change. He was still looking right into Catron's eyes. His own voice showed signs of annoyance now, building up like steam.

"Oh, yes you are, Phil. You're going to see her. I don't know what's happened to you, but I don't like it."

Catron fidgeted. He scratched his throat, then the back of his neck. He took the dangling cigarette from his mouth and ground it out in the ashtray, though it was barely used. Pinpricks of sweat were materializing on his face and forehead.

"I'm not going," he said firmly, hitting two typewriter keys. "For all I care, you can ride to hell with the devil's pitchfork up your ass and take everyone else with you, but this Bruja thing is out of the question. I'm not going."

Harmon leaned forward, nose-to-nose with the writer, and hissed, "You're going."

Catron pulled back, looking up past the face that loomed in front of his, toward the picture. It was glowing, a light literally shining from the canvas, a supernatural aura, bright and eerie. Words were coming into his mind, and impulses, ones he could not control. Harmon had withdrawn slightly, but he was still there waiting for an answer.

"I'm not going," he repeated.

"Oh, yes you are, Phil. You're going if . . . "

Catron picked up the ashtray from the desk and flung the contents into the wrestling manager's face. For an instant, the surroundings were filled with gray powder, the cold ashes and extinguished cigarette butts flying through the air. As they caught Harmon, he stumbled backward, more from surprise than anything else, his hands dancing protectively in front of his eyes. Still, he kept control of himself, in spite of the compulsion to do otherwise. Staring down at the man behind the desk, his words came out slow, a syllable at a time.

"You're going, you son of a bitch. You're going."

Harmon stormed out of the room, slamming the door behind him. Catron watched him go. As his antagonizer went out of sight, a warm feeling came over him, one of confidence and temporary relief. He felt the corners of his lips turning into a smile that wasn't his own, but a cocky half-smirk, mingling an expression of bemused arrogance with the undescribable depression which came from the soul. It was not the expression of Phil Catron in amusement, but that of Jaime Sublaran.

"La Bruja," he piped, the words swirling around inside his head like miniature whirlpools, before coming out his mouth. "You are still alive? How interesting."

He began to type, when he felt another unexplained presence in the room. Looking up at the picture, he was relieved to see it was as normal as ever, without further change. Again, he thought of the old woman and Harmon's warning.

"I think you should let this story go."

He shook his head in disgust and continued to type. He was going fast. It seemed like his fingers were doing all the work independently, without being activated by his brain. Amid the blur that came across the paper, between each stroke of the flashing keys, he could read the words: "I live. I live. I live. I live. I live. I live."

With a scream, he rose from the desk, knocking the typewriter and the rest of the desktop contents to the floor. Harmon, hearing the noise, came to the door, looking in with an expression on his face which plainly said he didn't know what was going on. Catron was on his feet, staring up at the oil painting, eyes wide and mouth twisted in hate.

"Phil?" he asked, entering the study. "Phil, are you okay?"

Catron turned to him, his mouth inching upward to form a smirk, half-arrogant, half-mournful. Though Freddie had never seen Jaime Sublaran alive, he recognized the mimicry from the pictures and grew all the more frightened.

"Phil?" he repeated with more emphasis. "Phil, what's wrong?"

"La Bruja," Catron whispered, his eyes glowing with a new and completely different light. "Give me La Bruja. Tomorrow, we go to see her."

# 11

# THE DEVIL TIMES TEN

Freddie Harmon sat alone in the parlor while Catron and La Bruja talked behind closed doors in her fortune-telling chambers. The room looked like something out of the gypsy camp in one of Lon Chaney, Jr.'s werewolf films. A circular table, surrounded by chairs, burning candles everywhere, and the old woman herself, blending in with these strange surroundings, as they questioned each other.

"You have the smell of death about you," she said flatly. "The powers of evil lean heavily on your shoulders. They want to possess you very badly. Do you have any idea why?"

Catron shrugged and put a cigarette to his lips, but La Bruja leaned forward and knocked it from his mouth with a wisp of her hand, indicating with all certainty she did not allow smoking on her seance time.

"My business is to be taken seriously or not at all," she scolded, resuming her position in the chair directly across from Catron's. "You are a man of free will. You have the choice to accept or reject my advice, but in either case I ask to be respected. I tell you, you are in danger. You are all in danger. I know whose house you are living in. You've got to leave. Go while you still can."

"Did you know Sublaran?" Catron asked out of the heavens, ignoring her words. The old woman stiffened, her face reflecting memories returned, which she'd preferred to have buried. It was then she noticed the charm dangling around his neck at the open shirt collar, a five-starred pentagram, and her eyes widened in horror.

"Where did you get that?"

Catron looked at her, perplexed, not understanding her concern. This wasn't working out. It was getting him nowhere. He hadn't learned anything from La Bruja in regards to Jaime Sublaran, but had only been pelted by warnings that made no sense.

"Why?" he asked sarcastically. "Does this charm smell of death too?"

The old woman's gaze was hard, cold, and anticipative, for she had known the matador when he was still alive, far too well. Now, after more than twenty years, the devil was returning to her, rising from the dust like a whirlwind. If there was even partial truth to the legends of magic charms, ghosts, and phenomena that she advertised so relentlessly for the sake of her business, then this man stood in the very face of danger, yet was too foolish to understand.

"That charm was his!"

Catron flinched, fingering the pentagram. Although he knew what the answer would be, the question slipped out.

"His?"

"That charm belonged to Jaime Sublaran."

"You mean you're familiar with it?"

The old woman closed her eyes, thinking back, and it became difficult to tell just who was advising whom in their little circle. Catron knew he'd hit onto something and tried to press the point further, but Bruja kept brushing him off, going back into her warnings about danger and pending doom. They were walking on a treadmill.

"You've got to get rid of that charm. Get out of that house. Go before . . . "

"Beware of what? A charm I found in a box in an attic, a house, a bunch of spooks running around in bedsheets, with two holes cut into them for eyes? Old woman, I was born at night, but not last night. Save your hocus pocus con game for someone who believes it and answer me straight."

La Bruja's face twisted quizzically, making it obvious she did not understand American slang. Catron tried to think of the words in Spanish but could not. It didn't matter anyway, for she was off on her tangent again.

"I forewarned Jaime Sublaran of his death in the ring. I could see it happening, the bull coming toward him, hooking into his face and neck, again and again. I saw it all and warned him, yet he did not heed my warning. You are the same way. You laugh in the face of death, yet you do not know how close he is standing to you. The figure of death looks over your shoulder and he is waiting to strike. You must leave Spain, at once. I know what is going to happen. I smell death on you and see it in your eyes."

Again, Catron felt the pounding in his head, just as he had in the front row of the Huelva bullring, when Montana was gored. He put his fingers to his temples, rubbing softly, his eyes closed. La Bruja was still carrying on, but her words were far off. He felt himself swimming away, to another world, another time. Like the old woman, he too was seeing visions, but his were evidently far less pleasant.

Xavier Cristo Cruz!

The words were large on the granite tombstone, which featured a bust of the late matador wearing a suit of lights and matador's hat. From his vantage place, Jaime Sublaran looked down on the burial sight and cursed. His eyes, hidden by dark glasses, must have been blazing, and an expression of suppressed anger twisted across his face. He was speaking in Spanish, but Catron was somehow able to translate the words.

"So you wanted to be a hero, to live forever in the minds of the fans. Now, you've gotten your wish, matador. Now you'll be remembered forever, just like you wanted . . . but not as a rival to me. I have no rivals. Next to me, there is no other. I have the power and no one lives who places himself as my equal."

Sublaran looked different in street clothes, a black suit and polka dotted shirt open at the collar. Somehow, he did not look natural outside the glistening suit of lights.

"If it's any satisfaction," he mouthed, speaking to the headstone, "I know you'll be happy to hear that the people are turning on me. They blame me for your death. Isn't that stupid? They blame me."

Suppressing a laugh, Sublaran withdrew a package of cigarettes from his jacket pocket, and put one to his lips, the last in the pack. Contemptuously, he crumbled the paper package and tossed it on top the grave. Before it was mangled, he had been able to make out the brand. The matador was smoking Celtas.

"Showers of blessings," he sneered, turning to walk away. "For you there will be no triumphant laps of the ring, no more ears and tails, and no more gossip that you will be the successor to my throne. No one sits on my throne, ever."

The great figures of the past had come and gone, leaving their respected marks, but all of them combined possessed not half the arrogance of Jaime Sublaran. Yet such would never surface while he was alive. Only in death would the gossip spread, the slander start, and the ruination process begin. Lagartijo, Manolete, Chilolin, Litri, Manolo Martinez, El Cordobes, Mondeno, Dominguin. All were remembered for the greatness they possessed and the honor they brought to bullfighting. But for Sublaran, a different fate awaited. Would he be remembered for the many glorious afternoons? No, he would be remembered for one day in Huelva, where his rival shot himself, and rather than mourn, he had laughed triumphantly. A high price to pay, perhaps too high.

"What's wrong with you?"

Catron opened his eyes. La Bruja was staring at him, looking disturbed. Suddenly, he was filled with an irrational loathing for her, and a grim familiarity with all his surroundings, though he had never been there before. His lips were forming a question, involuntarily, escaping from his mouth before he could stop the flow.

"What did you think of Jaime Sublaran?"

The old woman hesitated, not sure of what to say or do. She noticed the peculiar look on Phil Catron's face, the lip twisted slightly to the side in a confident half-smirk that almost resembled Jaime Sublaran. To see the deceased matador imitated in such a way made her shudder. This man was making her feel very, very uncomfortable.

"What did you think of Jaime Sublaran?" he repeated.

"He was the devil times ten," she answered abruptly, then wished she hadn't. "There was no good in the man, no good at all."

A hundred pictures flashed before Catron's eyes with those words. Cristo Cruz in Huelva being booed and jeered while Jaime Sublaran watched in the background, relishing the moment. The oil painting that had so captured his likeness. Paco Solorzano, now dead, and his words concerning the disoriented personality of his former employer. The opening sounds of "La Ultima Estocada," the Sublaran theme, and the ever-present Cat Walk, in the center of the arena, strutting and dancing in front of the horns.

Then there were other words, ones that didn't fit in, but vaguely familiar. The words of a sermon, the minister hollering and screaming before the congregation, warning of the eternal torment that awaited the devil's own.

"The Bible clearly states that if you are to see the kingdom of God, you must repent and accept Jesus Christ as your savior. You've got to turn from your sins and confess your need of salvation. There is no other way. The choice is yours. Heaven or hell. You can go with God or you can go with the devil."

"He was the devil times ten."

"You're just a crazy old woman," Catron screamed, leaping from his seat. His face was livid with rage. "I should have never come here. I don't need you. I don't need any of these people. The bull hasn't been born that can kill me, do you hear! It doesn't matter what they saw! It doesn't matter, because I have the power! I've worked all my life to get to where I am, and nobody's going to take it away from me! No one rivals me! They aren't better than me! They aren't! Damned be the lot of you."

Shoving the doors open, he rushed through the waiting room and to the exit. Freddie Harmon rose and tried to grab at him as he made his way out, but Catron turned and brushed him aside with strength that would seem unnatural for someone of his size and build.

"I don't need any of you!" he shouted. "I don't need any of you for anything. You aren't better than me. None of you are. You just think you are, but you aren't."

He was out the door and into the street before Freddie collared him. Catron turned and catching him just right, knocked the wrestling manager against the wall, screaming all the while.

"Lay off of me or I'll fix you, you son of a bitch! You all act like you're the holiest of holies, you rotten, stinking hypocrites. Stay away from me or by God, I'll get a sword and cut your guts out. No one rivals me. No one. No one."

He began to hurry away, walking fast but not running. Behind him, La Bruja and two passersby were helping Freddie Harmon to his feet. Still dazed, he was more confused by Phil Catron's behavior than by the physical attack.

"Damn," he muttered, trying to maintain his composure as he dusted himself off, "what did you say to him?"

La Bruja shrugged her shoulders, but as she watched the irate American storming down the street, another thought emerged, one the others were fortunate not to know. She was remembering a certain vow, made to her by a certain matador, more than twenty years ago, shortly before a bull crushed his head like a broken vase falling on the sidewalk. And furthermore, she remembered a sideways smirk, one that had remained forgotten until this day. Under her breath, she cursed her own luck and the other American, who had brought Catron to her.

"This couldn't be happening?" she mumbled. "This couldn't be happening. Not after so long."

In the distance, she could see Catron hailing a cab. Neither she nor Freddie Harmon made an effort to stop him. At this moment, it seemed best to let him cool down.

"What are you going to do?" she asked, genuine concern in her voice. "The man is deeply disturbed. I think he has a problem."

"Oh, do you really?" Harmon grumbled sarcastically, watching the cab pull out of sight. "How would you like to spend the whole summer putting up with this?"

For the moment, his thoughts were not on himself or on Catron, but on Dennis Flagstaff and his wife. Briefly, he analyzed the situation, then started up the steps of La Bruja's quarters, following her inside. For whatever it had been worth, the old woman had not yet been paid. As he reached for his wallet, he found himself thanking God, perhaps for the first time since he was a child and his parents made him say grace before eating.

"Things could be worse, I suppose. I could be Dennis, and that lunatic could be a relative. Lord above, thank you for not making me related in any way to Phil Catron. I'd sooner be kin to the devil."

# 12

# THE NIGHT VISITOR

La Bruja sat alone at the table where she had held her afternoon meeting with Phil Catron. The room was empty. Nightfall had come, and there would be no more customers. Yet this night, she wasn't thinking of her business. Her thoughts were focused on a single chain, a pentagram, which she'd seen before, long ago.

She closed her eyes, letting her mind drift away. Five years, ten, twenty, and beyond. She was no longer old but middle-aged, still possessing looks that many would consider attractive. The room in which she practiced her trade had changed very little. It was the people who had changed, the people and time.

"Tell me, Bruja, am I going to die?"

The voice belonged to Jaime Sublaran. Calm and chilling, as expressionless as his physical appearance, yet reeking with the evil that infected his personality. "What do you see for me?"

La Bruja stared into his face, seeing beyond, into his mind. Though the person before her was a living, mortal, human being, he possessed none of the traits that made him even remotely identifiable as a member of the race. There was no feeling, no remorse, no conscience. It seemed that beneath the flesh there was no soul and, if indeed one existed, it was so hideously depraved she was blessed blind to its appearance. The man had no fear of dying. If he was afraid, he was hiding it well. The manner in which he asked the question contained no notes of anticipation or terror. It was only an inquiry, as simple as, "Do you want me to take out the garbage?" or "What time is it?"

"Am I going to die?" he repeated.

La Bruja dropped her eyes from his face, down to his neck, and the shirt open at the collar. She could see a chain dangling there, not containing the commonly seen St. Christopher's medal or patron saint, but a pentagram. Bright with gold plating, the five-pointed charm gave off the illumination of a real star high in the heavens. This sign, however, was a symbol of nothing heavenly, but an insignia of witchcraft, demonology, and satanism. Had he the nerve to wear such a piece of jewelry centuries ago, he would have met death at the hands of the holy fathers, burned at the stake or died on the rack with a scream of confession on his lips, as his body was torn apart.

"The charm you wear will not bring you luck," she said simply. "I do not see death for you, but no good will come from this. I see . . ."

"Don't lie," the matador commanded, his voice still calm. "I am well aware of the source of my powers, as are you. That's not why I came to you this time. You have your God, I have mine. It is neither of them that interests me now, only the answer to my question."

La Bruja closed her eyes and concentrated. She could hear the noise of the bullring band playing "La Ultima Estocada," and see the bullfighter in a costume of black and gold dancing in front of the bull. As the animal came forward, he received it with the cape. The crowd was roaring, cheering him on, then something went wrong. A gust of wind, a miscalculation in timing, a loss of balance. It happened too fast to see, but Sublaran was caught and thrown to the sand, landing on his back. Before the others could come to his rescue, the bull was on him, hooking a horntip deep into the side of his face. His head exploded in blood, like liquid from a burst water balloon.

"Well?" the matador asked.

La Bruja opened her eyes, concentration broken. She was beginning to tremble, but the matador was relentless. He reached forward, grabbing her by her arm.

"I want to know what you saw, damn it. You know I don't have your gift of foresight. Tell me, has my power . . ."

"Deserted you?" she replied before he could finish his sentence. "A foolish question. Power from hell is never yours to keep. It is only yours to borrow . . . "

"But is it gone?"

She was stunned. For the first time ever, Sublaran was beginning to show fear. His eyes had widened, the ever-present smirk was gone. She could see the uneasiness in him, literally see it beginning to overboil. If only the fans could have seen him at the moment, seen the fearless king of the matadors in a moment of weakness. Though he tried to hide it, he was no longer capable. Jaime Sublaran was afraid.

"You don't look well, matador," she said, finding mild satisfaction at the arrogant matador's sudden change in tone. She knew full well that her words were churning in his mind, growing louder each time. He knew his hour had almost come.

"Power from hell is never yours to keep. It is only yours to borrow . . . yours to borrow . . . yours to borrow."

His lips moved, but no words came from them. His tongue came out, running over the edges of his mouth. He was shaking.

"What do you see?"

La Bruja shook her head. "I do not want to give this message."

"You must!" the matador cried, removing his hand from her arm and slamming it down on the table hard. "What do you see!"

"You are going to be knocked on your back. The bull will charge, the horn will catch you in the face, and you will be dead before you reach the infirmary."

Sublaran stiffened. He was starting to sweat. His eyes narrowed, then widened repeatedly, as if he was trying to focus on something that wasn't there.

"When?" he asked, pleadingly. "Where? You must have seen more. The bullring. The ranch or name of the bull. A date on the posters. Where? You must have seen more."

La Bruja shook her head, but Sublaran pressed, growing more desperate.

"The fair? The San Isidro Fair is coming up. Is it to be there, in Madrid, at fair time? Speak to me, woman. Ask your goddamned spirit guides. Ask whoever you want, but tell me. I have to know. I need more information."

La Bruja closed her eyes again, trying to focus on other details, but all she could see was the body of Jaime Sublaran being scooped off the sand, out of a pool of blood, men running with him toward the infirmary. One of the banderilleros carrying him had seen the destroyed face from a close range. He was puking, vomiting as he ran, though he knew there was no logical reason to hurry. The matador was dead. He scarcely had a head left on his shoulders. No one could survive such wounds.

"Goddamn you, I said I needed more," Sublaran screamed, rising from his seat. "Goddamn your superstitious gypsy traditions. Why couldn't you have lied to me! I don't believe you! You're wrong! This is all a farce! You can't see the future! It isn't true!"

"Then why did you come to me and ask me for the truth?" La Bruja sighed, opening her eyes. "If you don't believe me, then why are you afraid?"

Sublaran stopped his rampage, momentarily pacified. Standing erect, he once again assumed the position of an arrogant matador, afraid of nothing. The smirk was back on his face, yet the cockiness behind it wasn't nearly as blatant as before.

"I do not fear death, La Bruja. I only fear the ending."

"Death is not the end," La Bruja answered. "The flesh may die, but the spirit lives on."

Sublaran's eyebrows raised and his face puckered as he considered her statement, repeating the words, with minor variation.

"The flesh is dead, but the spirit lives on."

La Bruja nodded.

"The flesh is dead, but the spirit lives on," he muttered, eyes suddenly aflame with the light of old. "You know something, woman, you have reminded me of another ritual, long forgotten. There is a way, where I will escape my fate. It can be done."

He lifted the pentagram from his shirt and studied it, a grim smile crossing his face. He fingered the necklace like a valuable jewel. He was praying to it, as a Catholic would do holding a rosary. The words were inaudible, but the intentions needed no explanation. The blasphemy of a satanic prayer. Her warning about the powers of hell was forgotten. The man before her was obsessed, too far gone to heed logic or reason.

"No bull has been born that can kill Jaime Sublaran," the matador whispered. The expression on his face told her that no sanity remained there. "No grave can be dug deep enough to keep me imprisoned, even to the lowest depth of hell. They may bury me, but I will return, just like Christ!"

"He's coming back!"

La Bruja woke from her sleep, relieved to find herself at the table, with nothing disturbed and no spirits around her. She too was sweating, as badly as Sublaran had been when he first predicted his death. More than twenty years had passed since their final meeting, but she remembered it all, the matador, his demonic charm, and uncanny vow. Impossible. No faith spoke of a resurrection for mortals, at least in the way the bullfighter intended. Everlasting life, yes, salvation, and damnation, yes, but not like he had meant it. The meaning was too perverse, too demented for anyone to even consider. Foolish words from a maniac who should have been behind the bars of an insane asylum rather than in a bullring.

"Rise from the dead," she sighed, looking at the candles in front of her. "The wish of every dying man, to bargain for a little bit more of life."

The candlelights were flickering, though the air was deathly still. An odd occurrence. They were on the verge of going out. Thank God for electricity and the tiny light above the table.

Until this afternoon, she had tried to forget Jaime Sublaran and the prediction she had made about his fatal goring. Word had gotten around about her ability to see death approach. It had made her a local object of curiosity, one of awe and at the same time uneasiness. Yet it had helped her business tremendously. All so long ago, back with her now. The charm, the arrogance, the wild look in the eyes, only different, this time coming from a stranger named Phil Catron. It seemed as if the late matador had indeed returned, just as he'd claimed, but that was a silly statement, as absurd and impossible as Sublaran's rantings about eternal life through the powers of hell. Regardless of these facts, the day's occurrence had been an unnerving one. She was growing too old for her trade, starting to get caught up in her own fantasies.

Still, the remembrance of Jaime Sublaran could not be put aside.

It was not the look of fear she recalled so vividly now, but the gleam of conquest afterward, the face blazing with satanic triumph. At that moment, Sublaran had resembled more than a mere mortal gloating in self-confidence, rather the embodiment of total evil, no less than Satan himself.

An even more alarming question was posed. What if it were all true somehow, if a presence as imposing and vindictive as Jaime Sublaran's had managed to linger on from beyond the grave? What would it do, where would it strike if given the power? She remembered her own words, which hung in the air like a battle flag.

"Death is not the end. The flesh may die, but the spirit lives on."

Why had she ever spoken those words to Sublaran? Why had she comforted him, or worse, given him confidence. His expression had changed so abruptly afterward, from despair to ghoulish pleasure. What, in her moment of foolishness, had she inspired that madman to do? Beyond any doubt, she had started the warped gears inside his mind turning. She had unknowingly given a demon full power and a key to open the imprisoning gates of hell.

"They may bury me, but I will return. Just like Christ."

She could envision that matador, returning from the grave, dressed in a shining costume of silk and gold. Instead of scars on his hands and across his forehead where the crown of thorns had been placed, his scars were on the side of his face, a mass of them, a blasphemous duplication of Christ's resurrection. Rather than coming with arms open in an expression of victory and love, he came with fists clenched in hatred for all mankind. And he was laughing, as he never had before, even at the death of Cristo Cruz.

The sight of the tragic young matador shooting himself flashed before her eyes. She had been in Huelva that day, watching the bullfight when it happened. She grimaced, shutting the vision from her mind. "Too much to handle," she mouthed. "Too much to handle."

The only light in the room came from the lamp on the ceiling. The candles had gone out—not burned out but gone out, as if someone had blown them. The old woman stiffened, a word coming into her head, one word, which was feared the most, among all mortals.

"Muerte!"

She knew the meaning of the word. It was universal. *Muerte*. *La Morto*. Death!

She reached for one of the candles, bringing it closer. The wick was still there. It definitely hadn't burned itself out.

"Muerte."

La Bruja was jolted backward against her chair, her mouth cupped to prevent a scream. In utter, unrestrained horror, she saw the sleeve, glistening black and gold, felt the crusty spangles on her face, and the vicelike tightness of the arm clasping her head, holding her in place.

"It was true! It was true! It was true!" The warning erupted, again and again, but too late. From the corner of her eye, she saw the glitter of steel, a kitchen knife, poised in front of her face, and the hand holding it there, moving downward. She tried to struggle, tried to scream, but she could do neither. She was an old woman and her capacity to react fast had diminished, particularly when caught off guard. She had no choice but to resign to her fate, knowing her own hour had arrived.

"Muerte!"

The knife caught her above the left breast, sinking inward and twisting. A shot of blood spurted forth from the wound, then another, as the cold steel was extracted, the silver stained dark red. La Bruja jerked with the blow, her eyes rolling upward in convulsions.

The knife was coming down again, striking her, but she was beyond pain. In a moment, the suffering would be over and she, too, would cross the boundary between the living and the dead. It was not this fact that troubled her, as much as what she saw in the final, fleeting seconds, before her heart stopped pumping blood through her open wounds and blackness overtook her.

She had seen her assailant, at least a partial glimpse of him and had recognized who it was. Leering down over her right shoulder was the face of Jaime Sublaran, radiating with a cruelty that had been harbored for over twenty years. Just as he had promised, he had risen from the grave.

"Catron, come out of your goddamned stupor and answer me. If you don't quit cracking up I'm calling a doctor in the morning, and we're going to get your head checked out. You're acting nuts. You're rowing with one oar!"

The silence was predictable. Harmon, now nearly to the top, was having conflicting reactions. His logic told him to proceed, but his subconscious, that unexplainable part every man had, the part that was afraid of the dark, the unseen, and the uncertain, was screaming shrieks of warning. For a brief moment, he stopped, considering the situation, thoughts directed toward Phil Catron and his behavior. The arrogant bastard had treated him like garbage from the very beginning. He had caused him nothing but trouble by his escapade at the bullring, and had thrown the contents of an ashtray into his face. As a grand finale, there was the scene at La Bruja's, and even though it had been loosely apologized for, the apology just didn't seem heartfelt enough. Eccentric or not, he had overstepped his bounds one time too often. Harmon went up the steps and entered the attic, shouting.

"Phil, I've had all of this shit I'm going to . . . "

The light was on, but the attic was empty. Evidently, no one had been up there in years, at least from appearance. Cobwebs and dust were everywhere. Boxes, crates, and garment bags were scattered without organization, some open, others still sealed. As he took a few steps further, his foot hit something, which nearly caused him to lose his balance. Looking down, he saw the object on the floor and picked it up.

It was a plastic doll, dressed in a miniature matador's costume, an identical replica of the real thing. The only difference was the head, mashed and falling apart, where his or someone else's foot had stepped on it.

Unbelievable. It was the only word that came to the surface. The attic looked like a neglected graveyard, untended for years, but he knew that was impossible. Phil spent plenty of time up here. Doing what?

"Catron," he muttered, raising his head, "how can you stand it up here? It's filthy. What the hell is going on?"

In the attic's far corner, he saw a shape, partially concealed by shadow, yet distinguishable in the light. A glimmer gave the intruding presence away, the glint of gold-encrusted spangles.

Harmon moved closer, but the figure did not turn around, its back still to him. He could easily make out what it was now, a man in a matador's costume, black and gold, holding something long and narrow in his right hand.

"Phil!" Harmon shouted. He was only a few feet away.

The man in the matador's costume turned around, and in the light's reflection against the darkness, Freddie saw the face of Jaime Sublaran, returning his shock-filled gaze with a look of total disinterest. There was no surprise, no fear, nor even curiosity. It was a blank face, bearing no emotion whatsoever, like something dead and lying in a coffin.

Harmon backpeddled, but he'd only gotten a few steps away when the matador swung out with his right hand, in which he held a picador's pole. The side of the metal tip caught him between the nose and the ear, opening a cut as he was sent hurling backward from the impact of the blow. At that moment, he felt another pain and the air around him was filled with bright lights, which quickly collapsed into shades of gray. In the back of his head came a tremendous agony, where he'd struck one of the support beams, knocking himself out.

When one is unconscious, time passes quickly, for there is no sense of time. Like in the midst of an alcoholic coma, there are no dreams, no feelings, no recollection of anything, a nothingness which envelopes the brain and destroys the senses, until they are ready to be revived.

When that moment came, Freddie opened his eyes, memories of what had taken place coming back to him quickly. Maybe it was all a dream, something he would later wake up and laugh about over breakfast. If not, then there were other valid reasons. He had investigated the noise in the attic, imagined he'd seen a spirit back from the graveyard, and in his panic, he'd slipped, hitting his head. That had to be it. It had to be . . . but something was touching him.

Harmon squinted, zeroing in with his eyes. There before him was Jaime Sublaran, looking just as he did in the big painting, only more animated, without the trace of smirk or burning determination in his face. It was a blank expression, unlike anything he'd ever seen before, something from a dimension other than the planet Earth.

With as little movement as possible, he turned his head, to see the pointed tip of the picador's pole placed below his jaw, against the major arteries in his neck. Analyzing the situation, he tried to remain calm, cautioning himself, as again, his eyes drifted upward, following the shaft, to the hand and arm which held it, the torso, dressed in black silk, illuminated by the wire threading, shaped in a series of glowing four-leaf clovers. The chest, crowned with frilled shirt and necktie, the shoulder, and finally the face. It was still there, unchanging. Jaime Sublaran.

"You . . . "

Harmon started to move, but the matador pushed forward, driving the length of the spear tip into his neck, until the cross piece stopped it from entering farther. On the moment of penetration, blood shot out from the wound in a crimson spray. Freddie's hands rushed toward his throat, fingers clawed, groping the air and the shaft, but it was a spasmodic reaction. He was already dead, or so near to the point of dying that there would have been no way for him to save himself.

Still, the matador was unsatisfied, twisting the pole, so the point widened the gash, lifting his head from his shoulders by the jaw. He was trying to tear it off, literally decapitating his victim, but he could not and with a murmur of disgruntlement, he let the pole go, studying his handiwork as he stared at the motionless body.

Freddie Harmon looked like an uncooked piece of human meat on a spit, slumped against one of the attic's support beams in a puddle of blood, the picador's pole dangling from his neck. The creature observed him there, then shuffled off into the corner from whence it had come, returning to the shadow, as it whistled the opening notes from "La Ultima Estocada."

"Oh, my God! He's dead!"

Catron sat bolt upright in bed, casting worried glances from side to side. Sunbeams of morning light came through the bedroom window, and he sighed in relief, with the realization that it had all been a bad dream. He looked at the clock on the wall. A little after eleven o'clock. He'd slept late.

Falling backward against the pillow, he shut his eyes, thinking of how vivid and real his nightmares had been. First he'd seen the old woman, La Bruja, butchered in her studio, a knife driven into her more than a dozen times long after the first blow had killed her, then Freddie Harmon harpooned on a picador's tool. Even more frightening had been the murderer, in both cases grim and uncaring as any portrayal of Jaime Sublaran he had ever heard described.

It was then he noticed something else, a piece of paper taped to his bedpost. Taking it, he read the typewritten message aloud.

"Tell Dennis and Patsy I will see them when I return from Pamplona. Take care of yourself, everybody. *Salud*! *Abrazos* . . . Freddie H."

Catron crumpled the paper and tossed it to the floor, talking to himself as he disregarded the message.

"Pamplona. What would Harmon want in Pamplona . . . and I loved the way he told me about it."

As he considered the situation, he became less and less disturbed. After all, with Freddie out of the way, he would have the whole house to himself, at least for two more days. He would be free to do as he pleased, to continue with his work with no one, living or dead, to disturb him.

# 14

## MOON FESTIVAL

Dennis Flagstaff walked through Huelva's dimly lit streets, trying to avoid the passersby and the occasional prostitute who solicited him. It had been a long walk, hard for someone in his condition, yet seemingly impossible for a man who depended on his brain, rather than his body, like Phil Catron. Somehow though, the man was doing it, at a pace so fast it was difficult to follow. As he went along, trying not to be seen, he thought of his own words to his wife in their bedroom.

"Patsy, tomorrow night I'm going to follow him. The past two nights he's been going out, somewhere, for who knows how long, not making it back until morning. I'm going to see what's going on, where he's spending all this time. He's cracking up. I'm telling you, he needs watching."

His wife's answer had been blunt, uncomprehending.

"Let him go, Dennis. He's working on a book. That's why he acts like this. I know how he operates. Phil does crazy things when he's working."

"But something else is wrong. I don't like any of this!"

"Like what, Dennis?"

At that time he hadn't bothered to answer, but that something was Freddie Harmon. He'd spent over seven years with the man since his start in professional wrestling, and he knew his manager wasn't one to leave unexpectedly with nothing left behind but a crumpled note on typing paper. Harmon was a businessman. Articulate.

Precise. He didn't go anywhere on the spur of the moment. It had to be drawn up, exact, as when he'd arranged to rent the Sublaran house beforehand. He knew where he was going, where he was staying, why, and for how long. It had all been worked out before he ever left home. That's the way he did things, without variation.

He remembered Patsy's caution, but at the moment he didn't feel like listening to it. He was now sorry he'd ever invited his brother-in-law along, at his own expense yet. It was his wife's doing and now, having come to the end of his tether, she was still trying to hand him more rope.

"Phil's always been sensitive, so be careful what you say. He gets jealous easily. All his life he's been jealous and hurt easily. He was jealous of me when we were growing up back home. He was jealous of anybody at school who seemed to be better than him in anything. He used to think the whole world was laughing at him. He probably still does. That's why he took to writing. It was a profession where he could work alone, and succeed alone. That's why he gets so mad when you make your jokes about him being a pencil-pusher. He doesn't like you knocking his work anymore than you like him knocking yours. Just don't rile him, please? Be patient, be understanding."

Ahead of him loomed a circular theatre, the Huelva bullring. In the distance, he could see Catron trying the gates, searching for one left unlocked. He had to go most of the way around the *plaza de toros* before he found one, still unaware that he was being followed. Flagstaff waited a good three minutes, giving him time, then he too entered, finding himself encased in total darkness.

Following the feel of his hands against the wall, he found his way up the passageway into the patio behind the entry gate, where the matadors made their way into the bullring during the opening parade. From here, he could look across the sand, illuminated only by the moonlight and a lantern placed on the ground, and what he saw sent shockwaves throughout his body.

Phil Catron was dancing across the sand, a cape and sword in his hand, practicing passes. He was pretending to fight a bull, one that existed only in his imagination, a private performance before the many rows of empty seats.

"It's happened, just like I was afraid of," the wrestler told himself, opening the gate a little more to afford a better look. "This Sublaran business has taken over his mind. He's starting to go berserk."

He was desperately thinking of things to do, but the more he thought, the more he realized how hopelessly tied his own hands were. Catron seemed beyond help now. His games and writer's fantasies had taken over where reality once ruled.

"Jesus," he muttered, watching the whirling figure. "He's flipped, totally, wholeheartedly flipped."

Catron bounced back on his feet, then stood erect, tensing, regally arched in profile. The cape and sword were in his right hand, held positioned in front of him. With his free hand, the left, he motioned upward to the empty seats, toward the section where the bullring band would normally have been located, ordering them to play music. For a moment he waited, as if he could actually hear the sounds of "La Ultima Estocada" or another melody in his ears, then he started, one foot in front of the other, across the sand, toward the lantern. It was the Cat Walk of Jaime Sublaran, like he's seen in the film. Not an imitation without flaw, but distinguishable beyond any reservation. Phil Catron was Cat Walking, pretending he was fighting a bull, imagining himself to be someone else who was long dead.

Dennis watched in disbelief as the pseudomatador stopped, a few yards away. He was wearing his street clothes, the same he had worn all day. The only thing added was the cape and sword. From where he'd salvaged them he didn't know. The house perhaps, or somewhere in the bullring.

"Ha, toro," Catron called to his imaginary opponent. "Ha, toro!"

As if the bull had seen his movement and charged, Phil put the lure into play. He dropped to his knees, wrapping himself in the cape as he pivoted on his kneecaps, then repeated the pass from the opposite side, just as it would have been done in a real bullfight.

Dennis was shaking his head, explaining to himself what he thought was going on. "He can actually see the damned bull. He's imagining he's in a packed bullring, but he can actually see it all.

The bull, the people, the blood. He can hear the music, hear the fans cheering him. He's engrossed in this. It isn't a game. He's taking it seriously. He's actually taking it all seriously!"

Catron rose from his knees and profiled, the cape at his side, as he looked up into the stands, smiling. He was accepting their applause, hearing them roar with approval above the notes of "La Ultima Estocada." They were chanting his name. No, not his name, another.

"Sublaran! Sublaran! Sublaran! Sublaran!"

Possessed. The word went through Dennis's mind. Possessed. Taken over by a malignant spirit. No, that only happened in novels. Obsessed! That was the word. Eccentric. No, psychotic. Obsessed with a long gone character he'd made a game to role play. In this case, the role was winning out. Children did this sort of thing, swinging a homemade cape and dreaming of being the new Manolete or Sublaran some day. Professionals too, but they did their practicing with a partner in order to keep themselves conditioned. In Catron's case, however, it was pure madness. Grown men who were not directly associated with the bullfight did not play matador. It just wasn't done. It wasn't acceptable, wasn't rational.

"Why me?" he sighed, feeling sorry for himself and his wife more so than for his brother-in-law. "Why does something like this always come up? Why couldn't somebody else who deserved it marry into a family of screwballs?"

Again, Catron was doing the Cat Walk, more convincingly than before, with added emphasis. He was getting better at it. "Practice makes perfect," Dennis mused sarcastically, watching him as he fought the air. There was nothing funny about the remark. Not really.

Another series of passes followed and Catron turned on the last one, strutting away as if pleased with himself. The applause vibrating from the hands of a thousand unseen spectators filled the stadium. The band members who had ceased to play just moments before were hastily grabbing their instruments and starting up again. It was a different song, "El Gato Montez."

Catron raised his hand, shaking it in disapproval. He pointed to the bull, far away in the distance, then to himself, thumping his chest emphatically. It was his performance. He wanted his music, his theme song. Catching the sign, the band cut "El Gato Montez" short and again burst forth with the trumpet call of "La Ultima Estocada." A unanimous roar from every seat in the stands broke through the mounting tension, followed by a chanting, louder than ever.

"Sublaran! Sublaran! Sublaran! Sublaran!"

Dennis was tired of the display, having mixed reactions on how to handle the situation. One was to return home and not say anything about what he had seen, the other was to do likewise, only to alert his wife, Catron himself, and possibly a good psychiatrist. The third came from instinct rather than reason, to intervene and put an end to the eerie nighttime bullfight, cutting Catron's career as an imaginary bullfighter to an abrupt close. It was the last of these choices he decided upon.

"Time to retire," he started to say, pushing open the gate, but the sight before him caused his tongue to freeze, stopping the words before they left his mouth.

Catron had thrown himself to the ground, with such force he appeared to have been literally tossed and gored. He was lying on his back, staring up at the stands and the moon high above. Suddenly, he put his arms over his head, as if shielding his face from the horns, and began to roll across the arena floor, coming to a stop several feet away, to lie perfectly still. From the distance, he looked quite dead. There was no more movement, no noise, no sign of life. A gust of wind had come up, blowing a film of loose sand across the bullring, forming a misty screen against the lamplight. The game had gone too far.

"What the hell?" Dennis started to stammer, but again the words were caught between his throat and tongue, refusing to come out. On the ground, Catron was rising, pulling himself to his knees, then to his feet. Bending over, he picked up the cape and sword and began the Cat Walk all over again. Jaime Sublaran had been killed. His death had been repeated, but he refused to die.

"Ha, toro," Catron commanded, stamping his foot. "Come to me, pretty bull. Come and try to kill me. No bull has been born that can kill Sublaran. Come to me, toro. Ha, toro!"

Dennis thought of the home movie he had seen of Jaime Sublaran performing in this very ring, doing the Cat Walk and all the fancy passes, as Catron now mimicked. He thought of Cristo Cruz, crying and pathetic, as he leaned against the wooden barrier, while the fans vented their wrath against him. He remembered the horror-filled scene, captured on film forever, just as it had happened that afternoon, the new matador, would-be successor to Sublaran's throne, shoving a Civil Guard against the wall, grasping his weapon, and committing suicide, with blood-splattering, bullet-flying grace.

It was all coming back to him now. That night in the house. How his brother-in-law had insisted on running the films and picked that particular one. It wasn't an accident. It had been intentional. He could tell by the way he relished their shock and disgust. He had tried to hide it, but it had shown through like makeup trying to disguise a pimple or a sore. He was attempting to tell them something, all of them. It was more than just a joke. It was serious, dead sober, and mean.

He remembered the man looking up at the damnable painting following their argument, in a trance, asking the thing if it approved of what he was doing. He was checking to see, receiving thought waves from the grave. Possession, not from Jaime Sublaran or any other member of the spirit world, but by his own mind and his crazy fantasies.

Failure! That was it! His wife had warned him to go easy because Phil always got his feelings hurt. He imagined others looking down on him, making him feel inferior. Therefore, he had assumed another role, adopting the personality of a man whom he imagined to be more powerful than himself. By pretending to be Sublaran, he was making up for his own shortcomings. It had to be, either that or the impossible.

"Back from the grave."

The words made him tremble as he considered the possibility. Maybe that wasn't Phil Catron out there, impersonating Jaime Sublaran, but Jaime Sublaran returned from the dead and impersonating Phil Catron. He'd seen it before, in *The Thing*, one of those goddamned John Carpenter films that took the fantastic and made it believable. Whatever it was, was living in that house, waiting for people like them to come along. They'd played into its hand and now it was going to kill them all. Freddie and Phil were already dead. It had killed Freddie, assumed his shape, then went after Phil and killed him too. Now it had assumed Catron's personality and it was waiting for a chance to likewise strike him. Then it would assume his own personality and physical appearance, right down to the scars that crisscrossed his forehead from over a half dozen years in the wrestling rings. It would go after his wife and . . . he shook the thought away. He was going crazy, just like Phil, beginning to believe in the impossible so strongly that it became possible, nightmare turned to true life.

"Ha, toro," Catron shouted, shaking the lure. "Ha, toro!" Again, he stumbled, rolling on the sand as if a bull were after him, hooking with its horns and trampling him under its hooves. He was writhing on the ground like a pinned worm, arms over his face, head jerking violently as if something had penetrated his neck and was in the process of decapitating him. The seconds passed by, and he continued to sprawl on the arena floor, growing still at long last.

Dennis could take no more. He pushed open the gate and entered the passageway, crying as loud as he could. "Phil, wake up! Damn you, stop this!" He was about to vault the fence and set foot on the sand, when Catron rose as before, rubbing his head. Dennis repeated his words, shouting, but the figure paid no attention to him.

"Phil, wake up! What the hell do you think you're doing."

Catron took the cape and sword in his right hand, profiling. He was looking straight at his brother-in-law, behind the fence, but he didn't see, or didn't want to. Oblivious to his presence or his words, he raised a hand toward the seats, indicating he wanted music to be played. Then came the Cat Walk, slow, arrogant, a step at a time.

"Ha, toro. Ha, toro. Come to me, little bull."

Dennis backed away, striking the entrance gate with his shoulders. Stopping momentarily, he slid through the opening, withdrawing into the darkened tunnel. As he shut the wooden doorway behind him, he watched once more through the crack. On the sand, Catron was doing kneeling passes, the same as before, spinning and pivoting as he imagined horns slicing past his skull.

"Okay, Phil," he said in a low voice. "Play matador if you want, but I'm going home. I'll figure out how to deal with this later."

He closed the gate behind him and was instantly blanketed in darkness. He knew it would be difficult to paw his way to the exit door, just as it had been when he first entered, but he had to do it, had to get out and back home before Phil discovered him.

Discovery! The concern made no sense. He had given his presence away just moments before and had been ignored. The man didn't even know he was there, and he'd been shouted at, virtually screamed at. He was in a completely different world, apart from planet Earth, somewhere in the past, living the life of another man or having another man relive his life through him.

One last time he opened the gate and peered through, hoping that somehow the scene would be gone, that it had all been the product of his imagination or someone else beside Catron out there, proving a case of mistaken identity, doing a madman's dance in the middle of the night.

"Ha, toro! Now comes the end!"

Phil Catron was profiling, the cape in his left hand, the sword in his right, held at eye level, as he sighted down the steel blade. He made three fast steps, cape, body, and sword moving in unison, stabbing at the empty air, letting the weapon go. He turned, hurling the lure aside, standing alone, with his arms outstretched in an expression of triumph. The matador in all his glory. The bull was mortally wounded, as it was supposed to be, crumpling to a heap in the sand, blood spraying from its mouth and nostrils, choking out a final, submissive bellow as the last of its strength ebbed away. The bull was dead. The performance was over.

"Time to be going," Dennis warned himself. "He's made the kill."

Without another word, he stumbled off into the darkness, groping and clawing his way against the wall until he found the gate from which he'd first entered and pushed through. As the moon and the streetlights greeted him, he felt like Lazarus, raised by Christ from the tombs of a long dead world to the place of the living, where he belonged and was never meant to leave.

Behind him, Phil Catron stood alone in the center of the bullring, hands raised high. In them he held two crumbled pieces of tissue paper, which served as the ears he had just been awarded for his performance. From above, the applause of the crowd poured down on him like rainfall and the notes of "La Ultima Estocada" sounded like the fire of heavy artillery during war. First came the cheers, then the chant, as he smiled and accepted their praise.

"Sublaran! Sublaran! Sublaran! Sublaran!"

# 15

# WITHOUT PITY

Dennis Flagstaff had said nothing about the night's discovery to his wife, and nothing to his brother-in-law at breakfast or supper. For the rest of the day and the early evening, Catron was typing, until nine o'clock, when he made his usual disappearance, heading for the Huelva bullring to fight the dream bulls. It had been hours since he'd left, but Dennis had waited for him, listening, when he heard the footsteps in the hall. Looking over at the clock, he saw it read 2:30 A.M.

"Right on time, matador," he thought, rising from bed, carefully, not wanting to disturb Patsy slumbering next to him. He was wearing yellow pajamas, with blue polka dots designed on them. They were his favorite, but he'd never told anyone, nor had anyone but his wife ever seen him in them. Though comfortable, he felt they looked unbecoming a professional wrestler, let alone world champion.

"Now, matador, we're going to find out just what's going on."

The footsteps were heavy, almost a blatant invitation. He heard them pass his bedroom, pass Freddie's bedroom, going down the hall, until they disappeared. A minute later, he heard them again, only this time above, in the attic.

"So," Dennis said, biting down on his lip to muffle the words. "Now you're going up in the attic to play. Well, mister, we're going to find out what's happened to you. Brother-in-law, madman, or spook, I'm going to put an end to all of this bullshit."

He looked toward the bed, making sure Patsy was still asleep. She was, her position unaltered. Nodding his head in satisfaction, he reached toward the bedroom dresser and lifted a candlestick from the top. Without a word, he removed the wax candle from the holder and put it aside, so he now held a clublike, silver weapon.

"This'll beat your brains in for you, if you want to get rough," he told himself, slipping out the door and into the hallway. "I've got something to give you, matador, and it ain't a bull's ear either."

As he made his way up the hallway, barefoot, trying not to give himself away, he thought of Phil Catron. Was it really him, doing all this on purpose, or had he gone mad? Was it his own initiative or actual forces from the spiritual world, existing apart from the comic books and very, very malignant. Vindictive. That was a better word. Waiting in a dormant state, until they could be revived. No matter. Whatever it was, he had prepared himself.

The door to the attic staircase was open. He could see a dim glimpse of light. Whatever it was, whomever it was, it was up there, playing another crazy game, as it had in the bullring.

"No way in hell will you be able to understand all this or appreciate what I'm doing."

His brother-in-law's words. If he was a madman, he had pronounced his own sentence, incriminating himself. He had declared his hatred openly, hoisting the battle flag. This showdown had been building up between them for years. Now it was time. The breaking point had come. Everything had snapped in half.

"Ha, toro! Ha, toro!"

He thought of Phil and his burlesque routine on the sand, making a fool of himself, pretending to fight a bull—and be gored by one. He no longer felt compassion or pity, only disgust, which was turning into hatred. All these years he had known Catron and never liked him. Now he was certain. It wasn't a personality conflict or lack of understanding, as his wife had implied. It was more than that. It was pure contempt from his side. The man was intolerable. He didn't belong in Spain with the rest of them. He belonged locked up in a rubber cell, or alone on some island where he could type until his fingers fell off without being a pain in the ass to anyone else. It was going to end. Now. Tonight. The moment had come.

Slowly, he started to ascend the steps, the candlestick held in his right hand. Any demon or ghost who tried to interfere was going to wind up with a hell of a headache. He was hoping, even praying, he would find his brother-in-law up there, surrounded by dead bodies and a meat cleaver in his hand, just to have an excuse to pound the living shit out of him, then throw him out the attic window and never be bothered by him or his personality defects again.

At the halfway point, he could hear a noise. Whistling. It sounded like a march, or a bullfight song, lasting only a few seconds, then it was gone. His grip on the candlestick tightened. He pounded the end against the palm of his left hand, anticipating.

"I'm coming, matador. You better have your sword drawn because I'm coming to get you! The horns are coming, matador, ready to go right through your heart."

Again, he heard the melody, only it was a hum this time, more distinct. It sounded like the song on the record, the one his brother-in-law was always playing. He thought back.

"Sublaran had a theme song."

He strained, trying to remember how the song went, so he could compare, but it was beyond him. The humming had stopped anyway, leaving him in silence once more. He was almost to the top.

"This time, Phil, we're going to settle everything. You're going to get humbled, brother-in-law. I'm going to take all your smart-assed remarks and shove them down your throat. You hear me, son of a bitch! You hear me! This is where we handle our differences, lump them all in a ball, and settle them at once. You hear me, baby, because I'm coming! Right now, son of a bitch! Right now . . . "

Dennis literally leaped over the last few steps, rampaging into the attic to find it empty. The place was disgusting, full of dirt, cluttered boxes, and cobwebs, yet no sign of life anywhere. A draft was coming from the open window, but even the circulating air failed to drown the hideous, rotting smell, a stench beyond the mere odor of mildew and age. He literally fought the urge to gag, so strongly he was almost tempted to turn back. It was then he saw, at the other end of the room, a man sitting in a chair, facing away from him.

"Listen, Phil . . . "

The seated man didn't turn around. He didn't even move. It was as if he hadn't heard. Dennis studied him, calculating the situation.

"Asleep. Either asleep or passed out. Fine place to do it in too. The place smells like a sewage plant."

He moved closer, relaxing his grip on the candlestick. He didn't even know why he'd brought the thing with him anymore. What had he honestly intended to do with it, beat his brother-in-law to death? That was insane. For a moment he considered it time to leave Spain, early but safe. The trip was prying on everyone's nerves. It was beginning to show and take its toll on all of them. He sat the makeshift weapon down and went forward, unarmed. The wood felt rough against his bare feet, causing the floor to creak beneath him.

The man in the chair was sleeping very soundly, his head slumped down between his shoulder blades, oblivious to the intrusion. Dennis came up behind him and tapped his shoulder. There was no response, but the air around him smelled horrible.

"Phil," he said, shaking the man by the shoulder. "Phil."

The seated man slumped to the side, enabling Dennis to see the features at last. A case of mistaken identity, for it wasn't Phil Catron, but Freddie Harmon, eyes wide yet empty, jaws flopped open to reveal a cavelike mouth from which no breath came. Below, he could see a jagged rip in his neck, caked and clotted with dried blood, tendons and muscles protruding from the midst of the wound. Further below, there was something else, in the palm of the stiffened hand, a plastic doll, dressed in a miniature matador's costume. The torso was there, but the head was missing.

"Oh, my God," Dennis started to exclaim, whirling around in an attempt to get away. "Sweet Jesus . . . "

A silver flash came in front of his eyes, then the noise, as the metal candlestick caught him in the face, throwing him sideways. He could feel the tip penetrate as his flesh opened, and the blood spilling out, hot and thick. Knocked to his knees, he could see the weapon coming down again, striking him hard between the eyes, and a new flow of blood running over his face.

He had spotted the attacker too, a glimpse of him, dressed in a matador's suit of black and gold. He hadn't seen the face, only the body, glimmering with reflections from the dim attic lights, to take on a ghostly appearance like something from another world.

He started to rise, trying desperately to speak, but no words came. The blood was running into his mouth. He was dazed, battered worse than ever in the ring. His head felt like it had been broken into a billion pieces, screams of pain sending shockwaves through his nervous system. The room was spinning, whirling about in a mass of shapes and colors. Fighting, he pulled himself to one knee, and again the candlestick caught him. He had seen the blow coming, tried to block it with his hands, but the reflexes were too slow. It caught him on the left side of the jaw, sending him down, to land hard against the attic floor, his blood mixing with the dust. In his grogged condition, he could only lie there, playing dead, hoping whoever had attacked him would mistake him for such and go away.

He shut his eyes, feeling the pain swell about him. Words were running through his mind like tickertape in a machine, too fast to comprehend. All his suppressed fears had suddenly materialized, rolled together in a gigantic boulder which now threatened to crush him.

"I'm hurt. I'm going to die. What the hell is going on. Maybe if I just lie here, he'll think I'm dead and go away! I'm hurt! I've got to regroup myself. He's got me. I'm dying. I've got to fight him, got to live through this. Got to do it. Got to."

He thought of himself in the wrestling ring when he'd first won the title. He'd been drenched in blood then, too, but he'd felt nowhere near as much pain. He was parading around the ring, holding the belt high overhead, gloating in victory. He was champion of the world, the best there was, top drawing card, king of the hill. Freddie Harmon was running into the ring, throwing his arms around him, hugging him, the blood coming off his face to stain his clothes. They didn't care. They were in their glory, delirious with anticipation for what the future held. If only they'd known, both of them, they'd never have decided to give it a rest, to come to Spain and this damnable house.

A noise in the attic. If it hadn't have been for that, he'd still be safe, but he hadn't been careful, hadn't suspected. Now he was paying the price for his negligence, just like making a mistake in the ring. It was costing him, higher stakes than he'd ever dreamed possible. He had been beaten, humbled, knocked from his pedestal. An unseen assailant had done what no one before had even considered possible.

He waited, head threatening to explode, trying to keep from moving. He was counting the minutes, and the footsteps, listening as they walked down the attic floor and away from him, disappearing. Maybe if he had made a noise, if he could throw something through the glass of the opened window, Patsy would wake up. Patsy. It was going after Patsy. That's why it was leaving him. Patsy was next in line.

"Phil, why are you doing this?"

There was no time to even think of an answer. Oblivious to the fact that the attacker might still be there, Dennis lifted himself on his elbows, feeling the pain as his head swam and swooned. The cuts were clotting, but now with his movement they had reopened, sending new streams of blood down his face, this time trickles instead of gushes. He brought his arm up to wipe his eyes, seeing the pajama top streaked with red. He was to his knees now, halfway there. Ahead of him, he could see nothing. The attic was empty.

"Keep going," he coaxed himself. "If you're going to die, take that bastard with you."

He grasped one of the beams for support, pulling himself to his feet. He could see Freddie Harmon in the chair, head sagging against his chest, all but severed at the neck. He could see the attic too, covered with grime, spider webs, and blood. He searched the floor, trying to find the candlestick, find anything he could use as a weapon. He had to go, had to stop the madman. His brain was giving orders, but his body wasn't functioning in coordination with the signals it received. He put one foot forward and felt the floor give away beneath him. He was falling into a hole, into blackness. Then there was nothing.

"Catron . . . "

For just an instant and no more he could see someone looming over him. Yet it wasn't his brother-in-law. It was someone different, distantly familiar.

"Sublaran."

The face was partially concealed by shadow, but it was that of the matador, unmistakably. Staring down at him, heartless, expressionless, as if bludgeoning him to death was as routine a ritual as shaving or taking a shower. He had seen it, blurred against the dizziness and the blood, just long enough to make out the details before collapsing.

Unconscious, he had no track of time, but when he reopened his eyes, he knew something was still very wrong. He was propped against a stack of boxes, the blood drying on his face, his head a mass of swollen lumps and bruises. There was an object in his hand. Looking down, he saw it there, placed in his grasp by someone else. The broken bullfighter doll, the same Freddie Harmon had been holding, mashed at the shoulders.

"Adios, amigo!"

The voice didn't belong to Phil Catron, nor anyone else he recognized. It was deeper, with a Bela Lugosi tone. He looked to see where it came from and saw, heading toward him, the point of a broken banderilla shaft, splintered at the end into a wooden stake, like those presumedly used to kill vampires.

He tried to scream, but a hand was cupping his mouth. Beyond it was the gold and silk of the matador's costume and further up, the deadpan face of Jaime Sublaran. It was the last thing he ever saw, before slipping into eternity, realizing in the split second that he had been wrong all along. Phil Catron was an innocent man. A demon was loose, fresh from the pits of hell and hot on a rampage.

"Help me!"

There was no chance, for the banderilla shaft was buried deep into the socket of his left eye, passing through the opening in the skull and into the brain. A fresh surge of blood poured forth, over the banderilla's paper frills, covering the murderer's hand and sleeve. Though his target was dead, the creature was insatiable, turning the weapon, twisting it deeper. He began to jerk the stick back and forth, banging the wrestler's head against the box like a plunger, until finally the monster's bloodlust was filled and it let go.

For several minutes, the intruder stood motionless, studying the scene, eyes drifting from the corpse seated in the chair to the most recent victim, the banderilla jutting from his eye like a grotesque unicorn's horn. Somewhere in the scene, it found humor, because it started to laugh, a suppressed chuckle which held no signs of sanity.

"*Adios, amigo,*" it repeated, as it lifted the corpse under the arms and half-dragged, half-carried the battered body across the floor to the corner of the room, where Freddie Harmon was seated.

"*Poder! Poder en el nombre del Diablo, mi salvador y senor.*"

It set the body of Dennis Flagstaff to rest at the other corpse's feet, moving backward to evaluate its handiwork. A thought crossed its vacant mind, from somewhere, out of place. Laughter. Not his own. Laughter from another source. The creature shook its head, trying to recall the memories, but it could not, not at the moment anyway. There would be time. Patience had to prevail. Its memory wasn't functioning right. It would take longer. After all, it had only been reborn just a while ago.

"*Adios, amigo.*"

The creature shut off the lights and sat alone in the darkness, trying to recall its past and a reason for killing, the smell of death still strong in its nostrils, in spite of the open windows. Had there been enough destruction? There was plenty of time to get the others. Its bloodthirst had been appeased . . . for the time being.

# 16

# VENDETTA

Catron was at work by ten o'clock that morning, though tired and totally oblivious of any wrongdoings under the house's rooftop. At breakfast, Patsy had shown great concern because when she'd awakened, she had found her husband gone. Phil had tried to keep her calm, knowing how she worried about the slightest thing.

"Relax, kid," he told her. "He's probably in town. He was mentioning something about trying to set up a wrestling show in Huelva. He's probably out on business."

Yet it was past nine o'clock when she'd gotten out of bed and noticed him missing. It was now almost noon. It didn't make a great deal of sense. Catron considered this, looking up at the picture of Jaime Sublaran and shaking his head.

"Nothing makes sense. Nothing in this place. It's a haunted house, that's what it is, a goddamned haunted house. The spirits are lurking in the corridors. They're possessing all of us, making us act crazy."

He folded his arms and buried his head in them, resting on top of the typewriter. He was too tired to work. His writing was draining his energy from him, turning him into a dry well. The house itself was enough to pry on his mind and his senses, let alone the nature of his manuscript and the devil-man it dealt with.

He was drifting away, thinking not of his book or the bullfighting world, but something else, from out of his childhood. Dragged to church with his parents and little sister, being told to sit in a pew and made to behave. Though he was thirteen, they were still giving him orders, telling him what to do. Often he thought of the day when he'd be his own boss, where no one would criticize him or laugh at him, comparing him to his sister, Patsy. He'd show them all, teach them a lesson, prove himself as the situation changed and he was looking down on them.

The minister was ranting and raving at full force, a true, sin-hating, devil-chasing, revival preaching, Christ-exalting, hypocritical, arrogant Baptist. He tried to think of the name, but it wouldn't come to him.

"In order to go to heaven, you must confess Jesus Christ as your Lord and savior. You won't get to heaven by your church or your good deeds or by living a good life. The Bible says all have sinned and come short of the glory of God. It is only by believing that Jesus died for your sins on the cross that you might have eternal life. You must accept Jesus as your Lord and savior, now while you still have time. He is the only hope for you to see eternal life and escape damnation. In order to go to heaven, your name must be added to the Lamb's Book of Life."

"Lamb's Book of Life," young Phil thought. "Are we talking about heaven or a meat market?" He stifled the urge to laugh and his father leaned closer, whispering to him.

"You'd better knock it off, unless you want to get to heaven early."

Reverend Root. That was his name. Reverend Charles William Root. Conceited, smug, and boring, having long forgotten the fundamentals of Christianity, which emphasized love as Christ had loved, reproving them with religious doctrine and holier-than-thou cockiness.

"You say you don't believe in the devil. Well, you may not believe in the air either, but that's what you keep breathing, whether you believe in it or not. You think just because you tell yourself you don't believe in something, it's going to go away? Well, my friend, you are sadly mistaken. Unless you've said the prayer of confession and meant it with all your heart, God cannot save you. If you are living in your sins, without the blood of Jesus to wash you clean, you are in danger of going straight to hell. The devil has you, my friend, and only through the saving grace of Jesus Christ can you ever hope to escape his grasp. Satan hates you. The Prince of Darkness is a liar from the beginning. He'll trick you by giving you the treasures of this world, but he is quick to take back his gifts. The only thing he'll give you that is lasting is the fire of hell, and that will last forever.''

Reverend Root was turning red in the face. He was really going to town, now that he had everybody except Phil Catron listening to him and believing. He was pounding the podium, raising his hand into the air and pointing to the ceiling. His voice was growing hoarse.

"The devil is real. Hell is real. As Christians it is our duty to take up our cross, to be a witness for Jesus Christ and lead the lost to his saving blood and redemption. The devil doesn't want you to be saved. His greatest masterpiece is doubt. He's free to devour, because he has made certain nobody believes in him. Don't you understand, people. You have to read your Bible, you have to pray, you have to mourn for the lost souls. If you've got Jesus in your heart and in your life, you'll have the courage to face the devil, to see his trickery and discern your spirits. The devil doesn't want to see you saved. He doesn't want you to lead others to Christ. He wants you to be with him, damned forever to the fires of hell. It's your choice, my friend. Satan or God. Only a fool would choose Satan, but how many people do we know who have made that mistake?''

"Amen," the congregation shouted. Catron yawned.

"God doesn't need lukewarm, lazy Christians. He needs Bible-reading, devil-hating believers in the power of Jesus Christ Almighty. He wants to take you away from your sins and temptations. He wants to show you a better way. If you don't know Christ, friend, He's waiting to know you. Won't you ask Him into your heart? Won't you invite Him to be your savior? It isn't difficult. All you have to do is ask Him into your life. Don't be deceived by the devil's lies. He'll tell you that Jesus isn't really the way to salvation, that it's all a joke and the only way to succeed is the way of this world. He'll tell you all kinds of things to try and take your eyes off Christ. The Bible warns you not to be deceived. The devil is not mocked. What a man sows, so shall he reap. A judgment day is coming for all of those who run from the waiting arms of Jesus into the devil's hands. I made my decision for Christ many years ago. I was lost, but through Him I found salvation. I was taken from the darkness of my sins and made whole. It was through Jesus Christ, the holy son of God. It doesn't matter what you've done in the past. Jesus wants to give you a clean slate, to wash your record clean and make you a child of God. The only unforgivable sin is blasphemy against the holy spirit, to reject the gift of salvation through Jesus Christ. When you do that, you're accepting Satan as your God. There is no in-between. No halfway. You are either living for God or for Satan. To live for one means eternal life. To live for the other means death and damnation."

"This guy's going hot and heavy," Catron smirked, looking at the front cover of a hymnal in the rack. "He's gonna take that sword of judgment and stick it straight up the devil's ass."

Reverend Root was leading an altar call, inviting the unsaved to accept Jesus Christ as their savior. All hands were folded, all heads were bowed, except Phil's. He was looking around, studying the people. Someone was going toward the altar, an old man, and another one behind him. His father and mother had made that walk long ago. His sister had too. He was the only stubborn one, the holdout, the family dog. It had always been that way.

Every week it was the same. According to these people, you'd go to hell if you smoked, drank, danced, farted in church, picked your nose, or anything else except bowing down at the altar on some spur of the moment decision that would never be lived up to anyway. The routine never varied, a dull, meaningless ritual. The sermon was just noise, the opinions of a confused man speaking to an equally confused congregation. He longed for the day when he'd never have to sit in a church pew again.

"Don't let Satan win out," the minister pleaded. "Come and be saved. Don't let the devil hold you back. He'll tell you all kinds of lies, tell you your friends will laugh at you and forsake you if you become a Christian. Don't turn away from Jesus. Now is the hour. You may not have another chance. If God is calling at your heart, won't you answer the call? Don't let the devil win out. He'll lead you up a blind alley, then drag you into the fires of hell. Don't let Satan have the victory."

He looked hard at his parents, then his sister, head bowed, eyes closed, the picture of piety. He hated girls with that do-no-wrong image, that sickening sweet and innocent illusion. It was all a facade, a farce, just like Reverend Root. An absolute shithead, a turd from the shirt collar on up. He was still carrying on. His prayer was dragging, yet he continued.

"You've got to believe. You've got to have faith. The Bible . . . "

"The Bible is full of perversion, murder, rape, violence, lousy poetry, stinking literature, and stupid parables," Catron thought to himself. "You can have it if you want and read it, but me, I'll take something more sophisticated, like the comic section of the Sunday newspaper."

"Amen," the minister said, loudly proclaiming another morning of successful soul winning. "Go with God and beat the devil . . . "

Catron opened his eyes. There was someone else in the room, speaking to him.

"Phil, wake up. Please, wake up!"

"What the hell do you want, Patsy," he sighed, lifting his head. She was standing in front of him. Behind her shoulder, the picture looked down from the opposite side of the room, observing.

"The devil doesn't want you to be saved. His greatest masterpiece is doubt. He's free to devour, because he's certain nobody believes in him."

"Phil, do you hear me?"

"The devil is real. Hell is real." The words rang in his head. He was seeing over her, concentrating on the oil painting. There was no change in it. Not this time. It was merely watching him, listening to the conversation.

"Phil!"

"I already asked you what you wanted, goddamn it," Catron shot back. Patsy looked at him and frowned.

"You know I don't like to hear you use that word. You've been using it too much lately. If mother and father were alive to hear you, they'd . . . "

"Mother and father aren't alive," he cut her off. "Even if they were, I wouldn't care. Now what is it?"

She hesitated, looking funny at him, as if something was wrong, different in his mannerism. It made him angry. He knew he hadn't changed. Not since his childhood. They were the ones who had changed, always looking down on him, laughing at him, thinking themselves better than he was, though he'd made a name for himself and proven otherwise. They were still doing it, only worse. Finally, she had the guts to spit out her question. He was waiting for it.

"What are you doing now?"

He pushed himself away from the desk, stretching as he rose from the chair. At the moment, he wanted a cigarette, but he had none in his shirt pocket.

"I was planning on going up to the attic and work some more, why?"

Patsy recoiled, a grimace crossing her face. It made her look incredibly ugly. "The attic! What for? It's filthy up there!"

"It is not," Catron retorted, trying to get away from her. "It's clean."

"You've got to be kidding. I was up there the first week we got here, for curiosity's sake, and I couldn't stand going past the top step. There were spiders and bugs all over the place. It looked like a ghost town that hadn't been attended to in years."

Catron could not mask his surprise. They were talking about two different attics. He remembered being up there, doing his research. It was clean! Clean! She was lying to him. Or his own mind was lying! It was the house. No, it was her. She always lied to him. They all did. He wasn't sure of anything anymore. They were driving him crazy, making it so he couldn't distinguish fact from fiction. Patsy was looking at something else now, with even more displeasure. The chain around his neck. Her eyes were growing big, with a fierce look, like Reverend Root in midsermon.

"Where did you get that charm?"

Phil lifted it from his chest, holding it upward into the light, then in the direction of the oil painting. It had taken on a sparkle. As he stared at it, he was forgetting about Patsy, forgetting everything, but she was there. She wouldn't let herself be forgotten. Always pressing, always refusing to yield. She was right and he was wrong, unfailingly.

"That's a pentagram. It's the sign of satanism. Where did you get it?"

"In the attic," Catron replied, heading for the door. "I found it in a box in one of the trunks, up there. Is there anything else you want to know?"

She glared at him as if he were a total stranger, one whom she was displeased with, as if he'd walked up to her face and asked her to perform a perverted sex act with him. Now his temper was at the breaking point, uncompromising, unrestrained.

"What the hell was it you wanted anyway? Will you get to the point and quit worrying about my charm! What is it you came in here bothering me about anyway! You think I have all day to deal with your problems!"

"I was going to ask you to call the police," she said, pouting. "Dennis still hasn't come back yet."

"I told you what Dennis was probably doing," he shouted back at her. "What are you bothering me about it for anyway? I don't care about his problems. I'm not married to him. Leave me alone, damn it! I hope the son of a bitch never comes back. For all I care, he can stick postage stamps on his ass and mail himself to hell. He's a muscle head, all goddamned bulk and no brains. It'll be a blessing for all of us, if I never see him again. The more I think of it, the better off I am with the rest of you gradually disappearing."

That was it. The finisher. There were no more words. They just stood there, glaring at each other. The dam had broken, the truth was out. Neither could hide their feelings. The long implanted, mutual hatred had come through. It was Patsy who spoke at last, breaking the silence.

"You were always jealous of me. You were jealous of Dennis. You were jealous of everyone. Always trying to be the big shot, always the stubborn one. It was always you or nobody. You had to have the spotlight. Well, I still love you for the sake of Christ, but brother, you are trying me too hard!"

"And you look like a muskrat," Catron responded, pulling her childhood nickname from out of the past. "You're a real turd, sister. A real turd. People could get shitty hands just by touching you, and the same goes double for your husband."

Patsy screamed, picking an ashtray from the desk and throwing it at him. The missile landed short of its intended target. Catron smirked at her. He was starting to smile, enjoying it all.

"I owe you something, bitch! I'm grateful to you and the rest of the group. You brought me to this house and since I've been here, I've learned all kinds of things. My eyes have been opened. I've seen the light. I've seen you as you really are, still looking down on me, still thinking I need you. Well, bitch, I'm leaving. My debt is paid to you. I'm going back to the States and I'm going to leave you here."

Patsy was starting to cry. Her feelings were hurt. She was frustrated. She was outraged. What was making her brother act this way?

"I'm leaving you," he continued. "I'm leaving you to this house, and I pity you in its unmerciful hands."

She stared at him, not conceiving any longer. His words were rambling, a senseless bunch of gibberish. Had she pressed him beyond the point of no return? Had he finally gone insane, as she'd feared for so long? What to do now? What to say?

"Phil, don't go. We've got to find Dennis and Freddie. Something's happened to them. I know. Don't you understand? I need you."

"Good-bye, sister," he said, opening the study door. "It's just you and the house now. Take it up with Jesus, if he still has the power to hear you. He's a dying God, you know. He has no authority here. This is an entirely different kingdom."

"Phil, what do you mean? I don't understand you?"

Her face bore the look of utter perplexity. She had awakened from a nightmare of demons and maniacs looming around her bed, to find them there and a product of reality, not imagination. Catron looked at her, enjoying her bewilderment. Revenge. At long last he was humbling her, bringing her low. He felt like chopping her down to size, putting her in the toilet bowl and flushing the little bitch to the sewage plant.

"Phil?" she questioned, obviously waiting for an explanation.

Catron was smiling now, like a carved pumpkin on Halloween night, his face ignited with mocking pleasure.

"Just one word of warning, little sister. Don't go in the attic."

Patsy flinched, still not grasping the situation. Her face was a combination of all human emotions: sorrow, pity, anger, concern. He was toying with her, like a cat toying with a mouse before eating it.

"Why should I stay out of the attic?" she stammered.

"Because he's up there."

Patsy made a face. Another curve ball. She was striking out. The game was almost over.

"Who?"

Catron tilted his head toward the picture of Jaime Sublaran and began to laugh. He was still laughing as he left the study and headed down the hall, leaving Patsy there, alone.

"I pity you," he called out over his shoulder in a derisive tone. "He's alive, you know. Alive in this house. He's been waiting for over twenty years, and now his time has come. No one will stop him now."

# 17

# THE HORROR

Patsy sat alone in the vacated study, thinking of everything that had happened and, more importantly, a solution to handle it all. Her brother had stormed out, on the verge of suffering another nervous relapse. Her husband had gone off without telling her where he could be found. His manager had hightailed it to Pamplona without leaving a trace behind him. The whole vacation was turning rotten, like a half-eaten apple left out in the sun.

Her request to Phil about calling the police was invalidated. When she tried to use it herself, she could get no dial tone. The phone was dead. She could go to the police offices by taxi, but what if Dennis was in fact working on a promotional deal for wrestling in Huelva? If she went through all the trouble of contacting the law on an assumption that he was missing and he walked through the door at that moment, she'd certainly look ridiculous, more than she would care to.

"Don't go in the attic. He's up there."

Phil's strange words were vivid in her mind, making her think of a black-and-white silent monster film called *Nosferatu* she'd seen shortly before leaving home. The line was almost identical to that of another character, Renfield, a real estate broker who had unknowingly signed over a house in England to Count Dracula. Gone insane and turned into a slave for the vampire, she remembered Renfield in a madhouse, jumping with joy as a ghost ship pulled into the harbor, carrying a dead crew and the hell-creature's coffin.

131

"The master is coming! The master is here!"

The words were flashed across the screen as Renfield danced a lunatic's jig in celebration of the event. Catron, however, had not been as giddy. That was the scary part. If he'd meant it as a joke, it had been given in a manner far too straight-faced to provoke any laughs.

Patsy looked up at the painting of Jaime Sublaran, transfixed in her own right by the face that stared back at her. Cold and distant, she wondered what the matador had been like in person, what his thoughts had been away from the arena, and why so many people avoided mentioning his name. Odd behavior, since he had been the country's top matador for over a decade. It didn't make any sense.

A strange feeling fell over her, making her shiver. The room had gone cold, though it was a hot afternoon outside and the windows were closed.

"Don't go in the attic."

Yet that's where Phil was at, amid the rubble and the dust, daydreaming about a great book that he had not completed. His work habits had been unusual as long as she'd known him, but this time he was outdoing himself. She looked at the material on the desk, next to the typewriter. A manila folder, containing several pages of his manuscript, a reel of movie film, and a copy of *Paris Match* with a picture of Jaime Sublaran on the front. She picked up the magazine and examined it, though she could read no French.

"How strange?" she thought. The picture was so different from the oil painting. In this one, the matador was standing in the passageway of the bullring, his face toward the camera, brandishing a hideous smile. His face resembled a leering devil in an animated cartoon, teeth glistening with pleasure, eyes bright with triumph. Though Sublaran was obviously happy, there was a perversion about him that vibrated up from the very cover of the magazine, an aura of evil that was invisible to the human eye, but grasping, like a stranglehold on the soul.

She remembered the movie film, where Sublaran had registered such a great triumph, then moments later, the other matador had shot himself following failure. Again she looked at the magazine picture, seeing the matador laugh, a reflection of the sinister, unfeeling maniac beneath his outer surface. The story was coming back to her now, the one Freddie had told her when they were going by train from Sevilla to Huelva, about the circumstances surrounding the matador's last days, and how he'd jokingly hinted the house was haunted.

"This is going to be a vacation you'll remember for a long time!"

Until now she had forgotton about the magazine photo. She'd remembered the bit about Sublaran's fatal goring and Cristo Cruz, but the part about the *Paris Match* article had slipped her memory. Perhaps it was because Freddie hadn't dwelt on it or how the story had marked the turnabout in Jaime Sublaran's career. She picked up the magazine, opening it to the feature story. There were pictures, five of them, and the title in huge black letters: "Sublaran."

The first picture was a reproduction of the one on the cover, showing the matador laughing as he watched Cristo Cruz end their rivalry before it ever got started, by blasting machine gun bullets through his head. She stared at the photo, growing sick. She choked back the urge to vomit.

The second picture showed Cristo Cruz posed before the march of the matadors, smiling confidently. Around his shoulder he wore his ornamented parade cape, designed with roses and a big picture of Jesus Christ on the cross. He looked young, scarcely past nineteen, happy and anticipative of a long career in the bullfight world, one which he'd cut short with his own hand.

"Poor bullfighter," Patsy muttered, trying to decipher the writing beneath the photograph. "I wish this was in English."

The next two pictures showed Cristo Cruz and Jaime Sublaran in action, just as they'd been in the movie film, but a vast contrast was obvious. Sublaran, in his photo, was walking away from the bull, glaring accusingly into the stands. His expression spoke for itself. He was cursing the people, outraged because they had appointed him a rival, someone to share his spotlight, the one thing his ego wouldn't tolerate. Here was the devil incarnate. For the price of his own personal glory, he had taken delight in another man's death, the ultimate in abomination.

Cristo Cruz, in the other picture, was going in for the kill, but he was having a difficult time of it. The sword, instead of penetrating, had bounced off the bull's back, hitting bone. The stop action of the camera had captured the bend in the steel and the look of exertion on Cruz's face as he painfully tried to force the sword in anyway.

Again, she felt sorry for the young matador. Such a contrast between this photo and the one taken before the bullfight. Smiling with confidence then, he was now shattered. Dirty and covered with sweat, he was trying to kill the bull, but it was refusing to die. The final picture in the series told the rest of the story.

The body of Cristo Cruz was being removed from the bullring, face and torso covered with a red bullfighter's cape. The looks of the men bearing the stretcher were squeamishly unrealistic for those who worked with the bullfight and were accustomed to all types of blood-splattered injuries. This time, however, had been the worst. The unbelievable had happened, and it was becoming difficult to separate the crazy from the sane. Bedlam reigned supreme that afternoon in Huelva. At the same time a man had died, a scandal had been born.

"My God," Patsy said, shutting the magazine and putting it aside, "it was bad enough to have this on film."

She wondered what breed of man would keep such mementos around the house, answering herself before even considering. A sadistic lunatic or worse. A monster, absolutely inhuman, feeling no pain, no regret, only satisfaction. The magazine, the movie film, the relishing laugh. He had enjoyed it when Cristo Cruz committed suicide. Actually enjoyed it, maybe even prayed for it to happen. But what kind of God would answer such a prayer? Not her God, the God of the Christians, but other gods, false gods with limited power, the demons from hell.

"He's a dying God, you know. He has no authority here. This is an entirely different kingdom."

Her brother's babbling now made certain twisted sense. Jaime Sublaran was not just an egotistical, spoiled child masquerading as a man. He was not a malicious, envious maniac, but one of the devil's own, born again of the corruptible seed. The Bible spoke of such, when Jesus addressed the Pharisees.

"Ye are of your father, the devil . . . "

Jaime Sublaran was of the devil. She knew it now. So did her brother. Phil had known it for a long time, discovered it in his research or through one of the contacts he queried while at work. He had known, but had kept it all a secret. Why? There was something wrong, more out of place than it appeared.

"Phil, what's going on?" she wailed in a high-pitched voice, reaching for the manila folder. As she lifted it, the papers spilled out. She had no time to gather them. The title page told it all:

## THE SECOND COMING OF JAIME SUBLARAN
*by*
### PHILLIP R. CATRON

Patsy read the title, then looked up at the painting as her brother had done so many times and now her eyes had been opened. She could see the very same evil that Phil had, living on beyond the boundaries of death. A premonition had overwhelmed her, the thought that they were all in danger. Dennis, Freddie Harmon, her brother, and herself. She literally ran from the study, tripping over the chair as she went and having to fight to keep from falling on her face. She hurried through the lower floor of the house, calling aloud, but nobody answered.

"Phil, listen to me. We've got to leave here. We've got to get out, now! I can feel it! Phil, where are you?"

She tore up the steps to the second floor, searching all the bedrooms, but they were empty. It was then she saw the doorway leading up to the attic, open as if to issue an invitation.

"Phil," she cried. "You've got to come down from there. I'm scared. We've got to get out of this house."

There was no response, then she remembered her brother's anger. He wasn't speaking to her. She had to apologize if she wanted cooperation from him.

"Phil, I'm sorry. Please come down, okay?"

She was at the base of the stairs, but no answer came. He had to have heard her. He was just giving her the silent treatment, being stubborn. He'd done it before, plenty of times, ever since their childhood. Had they been back in the past, her parents would have slapped the hell out of him, but they were long dead and no one could prevent his pouting spells anymore.

"Phil, this is ridiculous. I said I was sorry. What do you want from me? Don't you believe anything I say anymore? Come on, Phil, I want to talk to you. I know you can hear me!"

Could he? Certainly . . . if he was still alive. But what if he wasn't? Had he gone upstairs and killed himself . . . or been killed by something!

"Don't go in the attic! He's up there!"

"Phil," she screamed, running up the stairs. She wasn't thinking clearly, her mind short-circuited with panic. She tripped on the steps halfway, falling forward, bracing herself with her outstretched hands. Pushing, she made it back to her feet and continued until she reached the top.

"Phil?"

The attic awaited her coming with anticipative silence, a dust-filled storage house full of memories and relics owned by a man dead over two decades. The place had literally gotten worse since she'd peered into it the first week she arrived in Huelva. Where before the place had been dirty, but with the semblance of organization, it was now in a complete shambles. Boxes were ripped open and thrown everywhere, pieces of different bullfighter's costumes were spread across the floor, and the storage doors were open, some hanging by only one hinge, as if someone had tried to pull them off completely with violent force.

"Phil?"

The windows were open, letting in a breeze, but the smell was awful, a sickening, spoiled odor that reeked throughout the room. She did all she could to keep from gagging as it hit her nostrils, the stench too much to cope with.

"Phil?"

At the end of the attic she saw two people, their backs to her. One was seated in a folding chair, the other in a broken rocker. Instinct told her what had happened before she had gotten close enough to see them point blank. She knew what she would find. The seated figures had been too silent to her call. They were either stuffed dummies or . . . .

Walking fast, she approached the two of them, reaching out to touch the one in the rocking chair by the shoulder. He slumped to the side and Patsy began screaming uncontrollably.

The blood-streaked face of her husband, twisted and gnarled in an expression of anguish, stared away from her, a shaft of broken wood protruding from his eye. Next to him sat the long-dead, propped-up corpse that had once been Freddie Harmon, reeking with a pungent smell where the black and bloated body had exploded. Under his chin was a jagged slice extending from the nape of his neck to the tip of his earlobe, his head more than halfway decapitated. She started backing away from the gore-covered corpses, babbling incomprehensible words amid the tears flooding her eyes.

"This can't be happening. It can't be true. It's a dream. God, let me wake up."

Something hit her between the shoulder blades, causing her to scream and leap in fright. Turning, she saw at her feet a miniature doll dressed in a matador's costume. Intact to the neck, the head was missing.

"Play me 'La Ultima Estocada.' Play me the song of death."

In front of her stood Jaime Sublaran, as big as life, looking just as he did in the oil painting, yet ghostly, silhouetted by the attic lights. He wore the familiar costume of black and gold, spangled thread glistening brightly against the dark silk. Around his left shoulder hung the traditional parade cape, which bullfighters draped over themselves when they made their march together into the arena. It was also black and gold, the only addition being designs of inverted crosses and pentagrams rather than the roses or pictures of saints other matadors preferred.

Jaime Sublaran, back from the dead! He had killed the rest of them. Now he was going to kill her too. Without bothering to think of how or why, she reached for his face, clawing at him, determined not to die without a fight.

The material her nails ripped against wasn't flesh but an artificial substance—rubber. As she tore away, the matador's hat fell off, his head snapped sharply, and in her hands she found herself holding a Jaime Sublaran mask. The creature stiffened, shock and horror mirrored in its face. Though it tried to conceal its identity with its hands, she knew who it was.

"Phil . . ."

# 18

# BLOODBATH

Phil Catron took the ornamented parade cape from his shoulder and threw it at his sister, the sudden flash of material in front of her eyes causing her to move away instinctively. The cape fell to the floor, amid the dirt and a dried pool of blood, the pentagrams facing upward. Patsy looked down at it, then toward her brother, not knowing what to do. He was starting to smile, not as he always had, but a grin—a sarcastic half-smirk she'd never seen on him before.

"Now, let me hear you laugh," he said calmly. "Let me hear you laugh." His voice was building with each word, growing louder, until it was a scream.

"You always thought you were so damned much better than me. All of you. For years I've lived with your laughing, waiting for the day I'd find the courage to do this. Now I've shown you, every one of you. You'll never laugh at me again."

Patsy backed away, then stopped, realizing the only path of escape was in front of her, blocked by her brother. She had to stall, even try to calm him down, until she could sidetrack him or manage to injure him severely enough to get away. She tried to talk, but her words were slow in coming. She had to be careful, for one mistake and he'd erupt. It was like handling an explosive mine which had drifted ashore after a storm.

"Phil, why have you done this?"

Catron looked at her and leered. He was enjoying this, having his fun before killing her. Somewhere in his twisted logic he was getting revenge for an untold wrong which she'd long forgotten, but that he'd retained and taken exception to. Again she asked him, her voice pleading.

"Why have you done this, Phil?"

"He told me to. He told me how. He helped me from the beginning."

"Who did?"

"The matador."

As he spoke, Patsy thought of her husband and Freddie Harmon, senselessly butchered. Nothing they'd done, real or imagined, had been deserving of this. She thought of her brother and how his behavior had been changing since they arrived in Huelva. And she thought of the oil painting, cold and looming in the den, hating Jaime Sublaran more so than Phil, for she knew it was the bullfighter's strange world that had inspired him, causing him to push himself beyond the edge of sanity. Still, she questioned, stalling for time, as she worked her way backward, against one of the closets, thrusting her hand into the opening, groping, to see what she could find.

"The matador, Phil?"

"Yes, the matador. I saw him, you know. First in my dreams, then alive, up here, waiting. He told me he understood. He said he'd kill you all for me, help me be rid of you. He understands revenge better than anyone. He showed me where to find things, told me what to do. The matador is here right now. He's alive. He's watching us. He knows when there's going to be a sacrifice made."

"But, Phil, the matador is dead."

"Oh no, he's alive. It's the killings. They're going to bring him back to life. That's the way it's meant to be. Just like Christ, he will rise from the grave. You've all been boons, blood offerings. Through the death of others, he can return from the dead. He told me so. He said he would help me kill you if I would help him come back. He is alive, in this house, a spirit waiting to be reborn."

Patsy grasped something long, a pole of some kind. Her brother was in a dream world, not noticing her actions. She had to get set, to be ready. It was almost time.

"You're the last one, Patsy. You're going to die now. You're going to be with Jesus, just like you always wanted."

"Phil, you need help! You're sick!"

Catron looked at her with a confused expression. He was thinking of the past, hearing his parents lecturing him, hearing the minister's sermon, and derisions from all sides, throughout his life. "Too loud," he mouthed, moving forward. "Too loud. Too loud. I've got to stop the laughing. You aren't better than me."

Patsy brought out the huge picador's pole, shifting quickly, so she now held it in both hands, the point at her brother's chest. She jabbed at the air, causing him to stop and retreat, forcing him backward.

"The game's over, Phil. The matador is dead."

There was no fear whatsoever in Catron's face, nor any degree of comprehension. He was staring at her, stupefied. "This isn't supposed to happen. You're supposed to die."

He could hear the laughter again, only louder, stronger than before. Patsy was bluffing him. The voices inside his head were telling him this, guiding him, as they'd been doing for so long. Biting his lip, he raised his hands, pretending to compromise, but he was only bracing himself.

"It isn't supposed to happen this way. It isn't supposed to happen. You have to die. Don't you understand? It's our agreement. You . . . ."

Reaching forward, he grasped the point of the pole and lifted upward, jerking it from his sister's hands, but the sudden movement gave her time to get away, slipping past him, under his arm. Before he could turn around, she was at the steps, falling.

"Patsy!"

At that moment, if a grain of sanity remained in Catron, it came through. Realizing what he had done, he too was running toward the steps, looking down. Patsy was at the bottom of them, her head on the floor, lying on her back. She didn't seem to be dead, but she was quite unconscious.

"Patsy!"

He started down the staircase but something was holding him, preventing him from coming to her aid. He heard the voices speaking all at once, telling him what he should do. He had to sit down on the top step and consider them. They were garbled, at times inseparable. He had to decode them, had to be sure.

"The flesh is dead, but the spirit lives on. There are more things in the world than what we see. There is another dimension."

"You're no good, Phil, and you never will be. Why couldn't you turn out like your sister. You're worthless. Absolutely worthless. How do you expect to make a living writing? No one makes a living by writing. You're stupid, Phil. You're going to starve to death."

"Jaime Sublaran lives on."

"If you enter the kingdom of God, you must be born again. You must accept Jesus Christ as your personal Lord and savior, or you're going to be damned. Repent. Turn from your sins and ask Jesus Christ into your life. It doesn't matter what you've done. Jesus will give you a whole new record. He'll wash the sins away with his precious blood, which was shed for you on Calvary."

"Don't go up in the attic. He's there!"

"Phil, you're the northern end of a southbound horse. I don't like you and never did. It's too bad your sister has to be related to you, and that makes me a relative by default."

"I'm going to kill you all."

"Why can't you be more like your sister? What's wrong with you! What's wrong with you! What's wrong with you! Why don't you answer me? Damn you! Why don't you respond!"

He could see them, no longer laughing. They were silent. His parents were dead and buried. Once a year he visited their graves with flowers, wishing instead he could urinate on the headstones. Paco Solorzano and La Bruja, cut to shreds. They could have exposed him, somehow, if the bodies of his family were found. Now there would be no way. He was sure of it. The voices had told him and they'd never been wrong.

"What the hell is the matter with you? Are you losing your mind? Have you flipped? You want us to call an ambulance and take you away? I know what's wrong with you. You're just a waste. You never were anything, and you never will be."

He could see Freddie Harmon just before the picador's pole was driven into his neck. He'd silenced the scorn and the subdued laughter, just as he'd silenced Dennis Flagstaff, justifiably. Now there was only one left. Just one, and it would all be over. He would be satisfied, having found revenge. The matador would be satisfied, now that the task was complete.

"No more laughter! Never again!"

Patsy opened her eyes, staring up at the flight of stairs leading into the attic. She'd expected to find her brother at the top of them, in the bullfighter's costume, waiting for her to come around, to be certain she was conscious and in full control of all her senses as she met her death, but he was gone. She tried to move, but the pain was overwhelming, preventing her from pulling herself to her feet. Awkwardly, she rolled away, onto her stomach, across the floor, then to her back again. It was at that moment she heard his voice, only deeper, sounding more foreign.

"I've got something for you, little sister."

She opened her mouth to scream, but the shriek was cut short by the horn of a bull, tearing upward beneath her jaw, at the base of her neck, lifting her slightly off the ground.

"Die, little sister. Die and be damned."

Phil Catron was sitting on her legs, manipulating a pair of mounted bull horns, the kind sold by vendors at any bullring in the world. He was no longer pretending to be a matador, but the animal itself, catching her under the jaw, just as the horn had caught Jaime Sublaran, one of the many fatal times, wrenching the makeshift weapon mercilessly within her, as she spasmed, kicked, and clawed, then finally went still. Blood had flown everywhere. Over the floor and wall, on his arms, chest, sleeves, and face, covering him with splotches of bright red. Yet it was over. He was finished and revenge was his.

"*Adios, mi hermana.* At last the laughing is over."

The right horn of the mounted set was buried in her throat, the tip plowing into her brain. She looked grotesquely comical, like an exhibit in the chamber of horrors at a wax museum. Catron stared down at the body, dreaming for a long time. He and his sister were staring over their parents' graves. It was Father's Day.

"You always hated them, didn't you?" Patsy asked.

Phil touched the top of his father's headstone, running his hand over the smooth marble, and nodded.

"Yes. But they always hated me."

"They didn't hate you, Phil."

"Oh yes, they did. You just never heard. It was always you or always someone else. Nothing I did was good enough for them. Nothing. Well, I'm sorry they died before they could see me become a success."

"Success, Phil?"

"That day hasn't come yet, but it will. Then everybody will have to swallow their words. I'm going to get even with everyone, do something that will make me be remembered forever. I never forget or forgive anything. Not ever!"

"Jesus said we should forgive," Patsy reminded him. He turned to her, his face hard.

"I said I'd get even with everyone. I don't forgive or forget anything. Remember that."

At the time the words made no sense to her. Maybe now, after all that waiting, they finally did.

"Let's go, little sister," Phil said, lifting the blood-bathed corpse by the legs, walking backward as he dragged her up the attic stairs. "It's time for you to join the others."

# 19

# PLAY ME THE SONG OF DEATH

Catron fell to the bed exhausted, still dressed in the bloodstained matador's costume. It had taken him longer than he'd expected to remove the oil portrait from the wall, drag it upstairs, and place it in the master bedroom. Afterward, he'd likewise removed the phonograph and the record with "La Ultima Estocada," which was now playing with all its blaring furiosity. Yet, as the song pulsated to a conclusion, he felt a certain peace overflowing him, and he was able to shut his eyes, drifting off to sleep.

The dreams were there, as always, taking him back in time, back to being a nobody again. They all looked at him with scorn, laughed at him, but now he had his revenge. The funniest part of all was it had been Dennis and Patsy's idea to bring him here to begin with. Justice. They'd chosen their own fates, for it was in this house the idea had come to him. Though the man was dead, the spirit of Jaime Sublaran lived in the hallways, forever walking and waiting. He had drawn strength from that entity, strength to do things he did not have the courage to do on his own. He had brought the matador back to life, used his infamous traits to infest his mind, possessing him, giving him power to avenge and to kill.

Now the killing was done. There was no further need for Jaime Sublaran or his memory. It was time to put him back in the ground where he belonged. It was finished. The purpose had been served.

"The flesh is dead, but the spirit lives on."

Catron opened his eyes to find himself surrounded by darkness.

The sun had gone down. Rising, he groped for the lamp at bedside. Finding it with great difficulty, he flipped the switch. As the light flooded the room, his eyes made contact with the painting and the record player, which had long since gone silent.

"Play me the song of death," Catron muttered, falling back on the bed. "It's my theme song now. I've made it my song."

At that moment he wondered why he'd done it, lugging the oil painting and the phonograph up to the bedroom. Impulse? Compulsion? What had been his inspiration for anything he'd done? The sword handler, the old fortune-teller, Dennis, Patsy, Harmon. In the case of the latter three, there was obvious motivation, but in the case of the former two, it didn't make sense. It was like two jigsaw puzzles had been mingled together in an attempt to make one picture, but it didn't work like that. Somehow, none of the reasons for killing Solorzano and La Bruja seemed justified to him now. They weren't that big of a danger and were certainly nothing to him. Only to Sublaran would these killings have made sense.

"Reparation? Rendering of accounts long overdue?"

There was a noise, a creaking above his head, low and scarcely audible, but there.

"He's alive. He's watching us. He knows when there's a sacrifice."

A noise in the attic. He remembered his words. He intended them just to frighten his sister, adding to his revenge by increasing her terror, but it was happening, actually happening. He'd heard the noise.

"He's up there!"

"You've all been boons, blood offerings. Through the death of others, he can return from the dead. He told me so."

Catron jumped from the bed and tore into the hall, finding it empty. He was alone in the house, the only one still among the living. His imagination was getting the best of him, playing tricks. He was beginning to believe his own dreams.

"Holy shit," Catron told himself, heading back to the bedroom. The seam of the matador's pants had split on him.

Again, he laid down, closing his eyes. He was almost asleep when he was jolted by another noise, louder this time, coming from above.

"Alive?"

The question hung in Catron's mind. He was starting to sweat, not just from the humidity of the Spanish night, but from tension, a shallow feeling within that told him something was not completely right. He tried to shrug it off as fantasy, like a group of children telling ghost stories at midnight, then being afraid to sleep. Just imagination. That's all it was.

"Jaime Sublaran still lives. All the power and the glory."

Another thump, louder still, directly above his head. There was no doubting this time. He hadn't imagined the sound. It was there. Someone was in the attic, moving things around.

Phil started to rise, then thought better of it. The idea crossed his mind that maybe one of them was still alive. No. Impossible. He'd seen them all. His sister's head had practically been torn from her shoulders. The bodies of Flagstaff and Harmon were so ballooned and black with rot he could scarcely stand to look at them. The smell was already infiltrating the house, drifting down from the attic to the second floor. It was a world of death up there and no one living could have gotten in.

"Just like Christ, he will rise from the grave." His own words, coming back to him, "He is alive in this house, a spirit waiting to be reborn."

He closed his eyes, thinking back to one of the church services out of his childhood. He remembered a Bible verse, paraphrased, "By your own words you shall be comforted and by your own words you shall be condemned." If that wasn't it, it was close enough, but he couldn't recall what the scripture referred to. Only the words remained.

Footsteps. He could hear them now, above. Moving about. They were pacing, just as he had paced at nighttime. Someone was up there waiting for him. The realization hit him like a cold towel in the face. In that moment the eruption came, an explosion of terror in its highest, most brutal form. Catron opened his mouth and screamed, one thought driving him. He had to get out of the house at once.

"He's back from the grave! It's really happened!"

Catron was halfway down the hall, when he saw the attic door open. Tripping over his feet as he attempted to stop, he fell to the side, landing hard on the floor. The house was filled with the sickening smell of decay, unnaturally strong, forcing him to gag. Choking on his own bile, Catron rose to his knees, then his feet, backing away as fear overtook him.

The attic door loomed in front of him like a gateway to limbo, the open jaws of hell. The hunger had not been satiated. The bloodlust was stronger than his own. Another noise was coming from above, growing louder. It wasn't a thump, but a murmur, the nervous sounds of a bullring crowd just before a bull was released into the arena. The sound was swelling around him. He blocked his ears hoping to cut it off, but the grumbling had become a massive roar of approval, the applause and shouts of *Olé* echoing through the halls. It was then an understanding came over Catron. The cataracts had fallen from his eyes, leaving him to see for the first time since his arrival in Huelva what was really happening.

"My God. You weren't my puppet, I was yours. It was you . . . all along it was you!"

He ran back to the bedroom, locking himself in. Behind the doorway he could hear the commotion out in the hall and the wail of the trumpet as "La Ultima Estocada" filled the air. Catron was in a panic, tears covering his face, mingling with the sweat. He was too scared to realize he'd stupidly trapped himself. Instead of getting out when he could, making a last desperate break for freedom, he'd been backed into a corner.

"He's coming back," Catron mumbled, sinking down to sit on the floor. "He's coming back, with music, cheers, and everything. He's coming back. Coming back. Returning in triumph to the town of Huelva."

Hysteria hit him hard as rolls of mad laughter poured from his throat. All had become a macabre joke of the most sinister kind. He began to laugh and laugh and laugh, even as the sounds approached, until they were right outside his door.

"Coming back," he coughed out between each laugh. "He's coming back from the grave. Coming back to Huelva, with his head busted open from the horns of a bull. He's coming back! He's coming to get me. My God in heaven . . . ."

The portrait had eyes, not slapped-on strokes of oil paint, but actual eyes, staring at him, full of hatred. The painting was watching him, coming to life. As the seconds ticked away, he could see the picture change. The flesh, the hair, the silk of the costume. The paint was disappearing, turning real. Jaime Sublaran was struggling to free himself from the picture, alive, starting to move. The matador was coming out of the canvas, reaching out to him. Catron didn't know whether the outstretched hand was asking for assistance, for him to grasp and pull, like a man being rescued from quicksand, or to grasp his throat and choke the life out of him. It didn't matter, for in either case the unimaginable was happening. Catron's deranged fit of laughter stopped. Only a scream proceeded from his lips, as high and shrill as a bullring trumpet. There was no longer anything to laugh about.

"Go away!" he pleaded, groping for the lock on the door. "Go away! Go away! Go away!"

Jaime Sublaran was there, in his room, alive and breathing. The black and gold costume, identical to Catron's, glistened an illumination of its own, supernatural, like the glow artists always painted around angels of Christ in holy paintings. He could see the matador's white teeth as he leered down at him, and the eyes, more burning than ever before. Had he the courage, he could have tossed the painting out the window or destroyed it somehow, sealing the doorway between Earth and hell, from which this demon had escaped, but it was too late now. Nothing could be done. There was no use to even attempt getting away. In sheer desperation, he tried something from right out of the vampire legends, joining his two index fingers to form a cross in front of his face.

"In the name of Jesus Christ, I command you, demon, back to the fires of hell. In the name of God, I take authority over you. Through the blood of Christ you are compelled to obey."

The matador spoke, but the voice was not that of Jaime Sublaran. It was the voice of Dennis Flagstaff echoing from the parted lips, pronouncing sentence, and the verdict was death.

"Jesus doesn't hear you anymore!"

Jaime Sublaran raised his right hand, a sword materializing out of thin air. Briefly, he looked away, as if into the unseen stands, motioning toward the bullring band.

"Play 'La Ultima Estocada!' Play me the song of death."

With all his remaining power, Catron let fly a terrible scream, then there was silence. Phil opened his eyes, to find himself lying on the bed, still very much alive.

Speechless, he could only shake his head weakly in bewilderment, knowing it had been a fantasy once again. They were growing too consistent, too vivid. Perhaps, he considered, he should seek some form of psychiatric help once he returned to the United States. Then maybe the dreams would go away.

"I don't believe this," he thought, getting to his feet. He looked at himself in the mirror, back at the oil painting, then in the mirror again. There was really no similarity between Jaime Sublaran and himself after all, except for the black and gold costume. Struggling, he removed the heavy jacket, letting it fall to the floor. The vest beneath and the front of the white shirt were stained with blood, which had long since dried from bright red to a duller rust brown.

"*Olé,*" he joked softly. "*Viva Catron.*"

The ordeal was over. Soon he would be leaving the house and the dead, along with the dreams, the fantasies, and the murderous revenge he had struck against those who had wronged him. What would happen when the bodies were discovered? He didn't know and didn't really care. All that mattered was this moment, not the past nor the future. The past had been avenged. The future was too uncertain to make speculations. For now only the immediate existed. Somehow, he knew everything was going to work out.

"A change of clothes and a shower is what I need," Catron suggested to himself, deciding it sounded like a good idea. "Onward and into a new life."

As he reached for the doorknob, he cast one glance back at the oil painting, which looked ridiculous sitting on the floor, propped at an angle between the corner of two walls. For a moment he almost wished he could take it home with him and hang it in his own living room. At least now there would be no little sisters, smart-assed brother-in-laws, or other intruders coming by to pester him.

"Been nice knowing you, matador," Catron laughed, opening the door that led into the hall. "*Adios.* What . . . "

Standing in the doorway, blocking his exit, was Jaime Sublaran, his face a fright mask of demonic delight.

# EPILOGUE

Carlotta the cleaning woman had a feeling something was wrong when she entered the Sublaran house for her weekly cleaning session and found no one inside. As usual, she set out to begin her cleaning with the second-floor bedrooms, but as she climbed the stairs the smell of decay hit her strongly, furthering her uneasiness. Nothing, however, could have prepared her for the sight she found when she entered the master bedroom.

On the bed lay Phil Catron, surrounded by a pool of dried blood which had turned the white sheet dark and oily. A matador's sword was driven completely through his body, the hilt protruding from his chest and pinning him to the mattress like a mounted butterfly.

As her eyes drifted she saw the portrait which had formerly hung in the study staring at the body from its propped position in the corner. At the bottom of the frame were Catron's ears, resembling either a grim sacrificial offering or mock parody of the bullfight itself. From what was evident, in the room, Catron had lost his mind, hacked off his own ears for some unknown reason, then driven the sword deep into his own chest. That had to be it. There was no other logical explanation.

Instinctively, she started to scream for help, but no one heard her. How could they. The house was empty. As Carlotta's shrieks fell into silence and rationality returned to her, she realized she would have to leave the house at once and get the police.

"*Madre de Dios*," she cried, crossing herself as she backed out of the room. "Mother of God!"

It was then she heard a noise, coming from above, the sound of footsteps. Someone was upstairs in the house and the attic door, which she thought had been shut prior to her discovery in the bedroom and which she hadn't remembered opening, was no longer closed.